The B**⚘⚘**B Girls IX

The Burned Out Old Broads at Table 12

In Training Bras

Rats, Broom Sticks, Snakes

A Novel by Joy Johnson

Stay up-lifted

Copyright ©2017
Joy Johnson Brown
All Rights Reserved.

ISBN: 978-1-56123-272-9

To order make checks payable to Joy Johnson Brown,
7230 Maple St, Omaha, NE 68134

Phone: 1-866-218-0101

CENTERING CORPORATION
AND
GRIEF DIGEST MAGAZINE
GRIEF RESOURCES

As the Mamas and the Papas said so long ago,
Dedicated to the One I Love
Ted, who inspired Raven
And for all of you brave enough to read the entire series.

That is BOOB Girl Bold!

Part One

Omaha's Long Winter

In the Bleak Midwinter

In the bleak midwinter, frosty wind made moan,
earth stood hard as iron, water like a stone;
snow had fallen, snow on snow, snow on snow,
in the bleak midwinter, long ago.

The United Methodist Hymnal Number 221
Text: Christina G. Rossetti, 1830-1894
Music: Gustav Holst, 1874-1934.

Never Underestimate A Burned Out Old Broad

The Long Hard Winter

It started in October. An unusually early Canadian Clipper pulled itself together in Alberta and rolled south with record speed until it settled deep into the northern plains, stalling, then taking root directly over Omaha, Nebraska.

At the same time, another low-pressure front said hello to the Clipper then joined forces for what would become known as "The Great October Storm."

Ice covered streets, buildings and trees.

Many of the trees toppled in the driving blizzard that built up and turned the storm into a real show-off.

Twelve inches of heavy, wet snow fell, its weight bringing down more trees, many of which hadn't lost their summer leaves yet.

Then another twelve inches – thick and heavy – fell.

The temperature dropped.

Marge Aaron, Mary Rose McGill, Hadley Joy Morris-Whitfield and Robinson Leary stood, wearing jeans and heavy sweatshirts, looking out of the floor to ceiling windows in the dining room of Meadow Lakes Retirement Community. As far as they could see were drifts of white, roads of white and a ground which was entirely white as well. Hadley and Mary Rose were wearing dark glasses against the glare.

"In the bleak midwinter, frosty wind made moan, earth stood hard as iron, water like a stone; snow had fallen, snow on snow, snow on snow, in the bleak midwinter, long ago."

Robbie Leary quoted the old hymn from the Methodist hymnal.

"Not so long ago," Hadley said, crossing her arms and squinting at the brightness. Even though huge flakes were falling, the sky seemed clear and the whiteness hurt her eyes. For four years now she had experienced Age Related Macular Degeneration, ARMD.

"In your case, ARMD means 'Armed and Dangerous,'" Robbie had told her when she was first diagnosed.

"No," Hadley had grinned. "That would be Marge."

Marge Aaron was a retired homicide detective and knew how to use a gun – or a red cane for that matter.

They stood there, best friends, shoulder to shoulder, looking out at the snowfall.

That same day, October 26th the mayor announced that for the first time in Omaha's history, Halloween would be cancelled.

Before she finished the announcement, snow had started falling again, creating a whiteout through downtown and in the suburbs. It was the same whiteout that ventured past the big window at Meadow Lakes, nodding and waving to the four women as it went by.

No one could go anywhere.

The temperature began setting record lows.

Children put on their costumes and little spooks and witches played in their own homes. Schools, churches and a lot of businesses closed their doors.

At Meadow Lakes Retirement Community, snow had blown into huge drifts that went half-way up the floor to ceiling dining room windows. For days, the wind chased its tail through the grounds, making the drifts even higher. The cars in the parking lot were almost completely buried. Zed Zonker's low-slung Thunderbird from the fifties was completely buried. Only the black top of the girls' hummer could be seen above the whiteness.

The entrances from the streets were blocked with drifts too big to drive through and city crews had given up on the street in front of Meadow Lake's big complex.

Everyone inside was trapped.

If there was an emergency, good luck.

Mary Rose McGill scowled at the window and walked back to her chair at Table 12. The others followed. Robinson Leary opened her laptop and brought Google up onto the screen. Marge Aaron picked up an outdated, folded Omaha World-Herald, moved her red cane to the other side of her chair where it hung over the back, and began reading aloud from any editorial that grabbed her fancy. Hadley Joy Morris-Whitfield continued reading a James Hankins mystery on her tablet and at the table next to Table 12, Wiley Vondra, Alphonso Greatwood and a new resident, Thomas Paul (T.P.) Roller, were all beating the socks off Zed Zonker in a lively, but relatively quiet, game of poker. Mary Rose leaned over and began to watch.

In just a minute she turned back to the girls. "Let's dress up like nuns and go to the casino," she said.

They looked at her.

"We can't get out," Hadley said.

"We're hostages to the weather," Marge said.

"Good try though, girlfriend," Robbie added.

"We could get nun suits on Amazon," Mary Rose looked at them and smiled.

"Shopping on EBay would do better if you want the genuine article," Marge looked up and smiled at Mary Rose. "And since when did you start calling what is worn by the Religious of your church 'nun suits' instead of habits?"

Mary Rose shrugged. It was going to be a long, long winter.

"This early winter makes me have OCD," Robinson Leary said, not looking up from the website she was studying.

"Obsessive-Compulsive Disorder?" Marge asked. She didn't look up from her newspaper either.

"No. Old, Cranky and Destructive," Robbie said. Hadley did look up from her tablet. "Hey! Get with it, girls. Don't be so negative. Winter will come and pass and it will be spring again. Just wait. The birds will fly north once more."

They looked at her and frowned. Robbie did an eyeroll. "At least we're good at multi-tasking," she said. "We can waste time, be unproductive and procrastinate all at the same time." Now they all did eyerolls.

"Who's being negative?" Marge asked, going back to Hadley's comment. "Now if someone tells me biscuits and gravy is not a good meal, I go negative and unfriend them."

Hadley leaned toward her. "You know what a pessimist is, girlfriend?" She smiled as Marge gave a small grimace. "A realistic optimist," Hadley said.

Robbie looked up and smiled. "I say when February comes, if the stupid groundhog pokes his head out and says there will be six more weeks of winter, we send Geoffrey out to kill and eat him."

Geoffrey, Mary Rose McGill's oversized mastiff, had given up on the snow as well. He, along with the other dogs who loved and lived with the residents of Meadow Lakes, had romped and enjoyed the first snowfall, tolerated the second and refused to cross the threshold into the cold when the third one blew in. They had to be pushed, led, or thrown out to go into the drifts. With Geoffrey, it required Marge and Mary Rose pushing on his hindquarters, then closing the door the second his last hind leg hit the snow.

Twice they shut his tail in the door, which made him jump and actually get into the snow quicker.

Now Geoffrey was trapped, too. When maintenance shoveled an open space for the dogs just outside the doors, it was covered with new, blowing snow almost before they finished.

Mary Rose got into the spirit. "Remember, girls, what doesn't kill you makes you stronger."

"Except for bears," Hadley added quietly. "Bears will kill you."

Mary Rose thought for a minute longer. "OK. We wade through all this snow to the chicken yard, get four chickens and bring them inside. Then we paint 1, 2, 3 and 5 on them. We turn them loose in the lobby and watch Alphonso and the guys playing cards at the next table hunt for number 4."

"Mary Rose McGill, you have changed!" Hadley said.

Robbie looked at her, "Who are you, strange lady, and what have you done with our sweet Catholic girl?"

Marge snickered.

Mary Rose looked serious, almost depressed.

"Actually, I was thinking about the fashion show we had with the Winkies nightwear and how Willie Winkie was always talking about how important our pasts were. Well, I've been thinking about my past and my growing up and it just isn't very nice."

"It's true we shouldn't live in the past," Marge said. "But the music was so much better then."

Everyone laughed except Mary Rose.

She got up and walked away.

They looked after her as she disappeared down the hall.

"That was sudden," Hadley said, turning back to the girls at the table.

Laughter from the poker players rolled gently over them.

Wiley Vondra leaned his chair back and looked at the three women at Table 12. "She's just bored," he said, nodding toward the door through which Mary Rose McGill had vanished.

He looked back at the man across from him, T.P. Roller. "T.P. here just got a new hearing aide." T.P. looked up, smiled and nodded.

"Good for you, T.P." Hadley said. "What kind is it?"
T.P. looked at his watch. "Two-thirty," he said.

"Ooooh kay," Marge smiled. "We'll see how that
works for him."

"Helps the poker game," Wiley said, and he rose from
his chair and wandered down the hall after Mary
Rose.

Before its Time

They held movie marathons in Hadley's apartment.

"If I see one more Sean Connery movie I'm going to go crazy," Mary Rose said.

"It's Johnny Depp for me," Robbie added. "Never thought I'd get tired of pirates, but I have."

"I'm through with Downtown Abby reruns," Hadley said.

"That leaves me free to pick movies with car chases," Marge grinned. "But I don't need any more popcorn with M&Ms and Goldfish crackers."

"We drank all the champagne that goes with it anyway," Hadley said.

They invited the men to play Monopoly.

They played old fashioned Monopoly, Star Wars Monopoly and Big Bang Theory Monopoly. Mary Rose McGill was the Big Bang champion and she claimed it was because she chose Amy's tiara for a playing piece. Wiley had Leonard's glasses for his piece and usually came in last. Hadley always grabbed Penny's wine glass.

Robbie was stuck with Raj's dog, Cinnamon. Robbie loved Cinnamon.

Hadley tried to teach them to play bridge. They failed. They also failed at everything but poker.

Alphonso Greatwood, Meadow Lake's owner, went out on a limb and organized races in the underground garage of the retirement community. While Meadow Lakes was an independent living complex, on occasion there were wheelchairs, walkers and scooters in the dining area and coming down the halls as knees and hips were replaced and just plain old age took over.

There were handicapped scooter races. Since only two scooters were available besides Alphonso's, he loaned his to Marge, who made a bad start by hitting the reverse button and barely missing Sledge Hammer, another retired detective. Sledge claimed it was jealousy and revenge. Marge claimed Alphonso had a faulty reverse button.

Cops!

Three out of four scooter races were won by Harriet Hill, who put a Go Big Red Nebraska flag on her scooter and left everyone, literally, in her dust.

The wheelchair race went to Howard Harr, whose nickname, of course, was Hardy. One again, Alphonso came through, finding two well-used wheelchairs in storage.

A large lady named Bertha Dee Blews took the prize - two bananas, in the speedy walker marathon, Bertha Dee's awesomeness jiggled all the way to the finish line.

Geoffrey led the barkings and howlings of the resident dogs attending the races. Everyone had a good time.

And the snow kept falling.

One afternoon they met at four o'clock for wine and cheese. Alphonso provided the wine. Everyone else brought different cheeses and breads and crackers and whatever was still in their cupboards and refrigerators.

The wine glasses sparkled in the afternoon sun as they sat around Hadley's table. For once, there were no snowflakes in the air and every so often the sound of one of the huge snow blowers drifted in through the closed windows.

Wiley picked up his glass and looked at it. The wine seemed to twinkle as it waited for him to take a sip.

"I hate to get technical," he said. "But chemists say wine actually is a solution." He took a swallow. "It isn't the solution to every problem, but then, neither is cranberry juice."

Hadley smiled at him and then at Alphonso. "A good man can make you feel strong and beautiful and able to do anything." She slapped Alphonso's arm. "Oh, I'm sorry! That's wine! Wine does that!" The two men groaned.

"I look at it this way," Mary Rose said, "wine is technically spirits. Therefore, when I have a glass of wine, I become spiritual."

Alphonso grinned. His scooter was in a corner and he was sitting at the head of the table. "I don't drink much," he said seriously, "but when I do, I turn into another person and that person drinks a lot!" He laughed his deep, resonant laugh and raised his glass to meet Wiley's.

Robbie was next. "I wrote a note that said, 'Dear Wine, you promised to make me funny, beautiful and a better dancer. I saw the video. We need to talk."

They laughed some more.

"I saw a great sign once," Marge added. "It said, 'I'm having salad for dinner. OK, it's actually a fruit salad.

Mostly grapes. OK all grapes. Fermented grapes. I'm having wine for dinner.'" They laughed again. Marge's cane was, as usual, hooked over the back of her chair.

Alphonso ended the wine jokes. "How about with all our talk about being bored and being negative, we say that the people who say their glass is half empty or half full miss the point. The glass is just ready to be refilled."

"Wait!" Mary Rose said, bouncing a little in her chair. "I have one more joke. I have a toast." She sat up straight and cleared her throat. "I don't drink much, two at the most. Three, I'm under the table and four, I'm under the host."

She blushed and looked at Wiley, who winked and grinned at her.

"Mary Rose McGill!" Hadley said.

Both Marge and Robbie laughed and did eyerolls.

Geoffrey stood by the window, looking out. As he watched and his people continued to talk, a gentle snow began to fall. The snow blowers stopped.

Part Two

Double, Toil and Trouble

Round about the cauldron go;
In the poison'd entrails throw.
Toad, that under cold stone
Days and nights has thirty-one
Swelter'd venom sleeping got,
Boil thou first in the charmed pot.

Double, double, toil and trouble;
Fire burn, and cauldron bubble.

Act Four, Scene One
The Three Witches
Macbeth
William Shakespeare, 1606

Never Underestimate A Burned Out Old Broad

The Girls

They were the Burned Out Old Broads at Table 12, named nine years ago by a skinny, feisty, retired Sandhills rancher with what she called "wash and wear hair."

Maggie Patten had put five shots into her mean-talking, mean-spirited, just plain mean husband's gravestone, taught them how to drive a Hummer pulling a trailer, and then had died quietly and fuss-free on a cruise down the west coast. The girls strapped her luggage around her and gave her a burial at sea.

They had loved Maggie.

After she died, her chair at Table 12 didn't stay empty long. Calamity Doodles, a spy, had finally earned their love. Esmeralda St. Benedict had taken them to Fort Robinson in outstate Nebraska, where the gypsy sorceress had led them to dream themselves back into the history of the fort and find parts of their souls. Then, Marge Aaron, retired homicide detective had arrived….and stayed.

The four BOOB Girls at Table 12 loved each other, took care of each other and were totally comfortable together.

It was all about the friendship of women.

Hadley Joy Morris-Whitfield put on her reading glasses after the wine and cheese party. They were the ones with the multi-colored frames. She pulled a small magnifying glass out of her pocket and began to read the old newspaper she had rescued from Table 12. Hadley was tall, stately and had more money than God. She had married well, liked big men, big cars and big dogs. She had an impressive collection of pantsuits and jeans and had been a professional volunteer and socialite.

Her husband, not always the most faithful, had loved her and shown her off as if she were a young trophy wife. He had died when his private plane that he was piloting crashed into the side of a mountain. She had one son who had gone through three wives and was still with number four. Hadley always said the unhealthiest and most dangerous thing he ever ate was wedding cake.

Hadley had loved an Indian sheriff, Wes Longbow, who had died the year before. She missed Wes. She missed her husband, too, for that matter. But that was just life and she was aware that with every day, all of us on earth are one day closer to our own death. She never took anything for granted anymore and every day, as she walked down the long hall at Meadow Lakes Retirement Community on her way to the dining room and her friends, she whispered a mantra to herself:

> *Ever this day, I resolve*
> *To find bits of happiness*
> *To laugh*
> *To recognize joy and beauty*
> *And to live a life of gratitude*
> *for I am a lucky, happy woman.*

And it was true. She was a lucky, happy woman.

No one goes through life always happy. There are ups and downs. Most people describe life as a roller coaster, but Hadley liked the idea of the spinning barrel they used to have at carnivals when she was growing up. You were strapped to the inside of the barrel. It began to spin. It spun faster and faster, then the floor dropped off and centrifugal force held you against the wall. When it was over, you staggered outside and threw up.

Yep. Life was like the Barrel Spin.

Mary Rose McGill went back to her apartment after the wine and cheese, Geoffrey trailing along beside her.

She sighed, lay down on her bed and patted the space next to her. Geoffrey was so big he didn't jump up to be with her, he just stepped up. He snuggled in with the lady who owned him. She put an arm over his big, warm body and they both went to sleep. Naps were no longer a luxury, they were a necessity.

Mary Rose had four daughters. All of them had "Mary" as their first name. "What can I say?" Mary Rose told people. "I'm Catholic!"

After their father died, the girls had moved their mother into Meadow Lakes without even asking if she wanted to go. She was overweight and dowdy with fourteen housedresses and two pairs of ugly shoes. But after being at Table 12, with three other women who saw her as she COULD be and related to her as she could be, Mary Rose tossed her dresses down the garbage shoot, went to Target with the girls and came away with a new wardrobe. Peyton Claireborne, Omaha's best stylist, styled her hair, dyed it blonde and she ended up wearing red rimmed glasses, all because of the friendship of women.

It was Mary Rose who always said, "Older women are beautiful! Just look at us! Our faces are sculpted and chiseled by joy and sorrow, tears and laughter. Our hair is blown thin by winds of experience and there is so much knowledge and wisdom in our heads, our heads can't hold it all. It has to trickle down through the rest of our bodies and that's why we get thicker as we age.""

She had also gotten the girls to say in their mirror every day, "I feel pretty." She believed "pretty" was a word older women had let get away from them, and older women are pretty.

Now her only concern was this nagging voice that kept reminding her of her past. She wished it would shut up.

Your past is always with you,
You are your past.

And a second voice whispered, *Make the most of it. Use it.*

Robinson Leary, PhD walked slowly back to her apartment as well. The wine and cheese party had been fun; the visiting was lively, the laughter natural and real. Of all the friends, Robbie was perhaps the most appreciative and grateful person. She was afraid she would outlive her money and, because of that, she made the most of every day.

Her unlocked door opened silently and Robinson went inside. Her parents had never locked their doors in their neighborhood of all black residents, and she felt totally safe at Meadow Lakes even though, just over a year ago, the evil Dr. Fell had slipped in at night and cut a large swag out of her hair. Dr. Fell was trying to kill Willie Winkie and he would have been happy to do away with all the girls as well.

It hadn't stopped Robbie from leaving her door unlocked.

"If someone breaks into my apartment and starts looking for money, I'll get up and help him look," she had told Hadley one evening as she watched her friend lock her door behind them.

Robbie went to a little hutch in her living room and opened the door. She pulled out a huge album. She sighed and closed the hutch door.

Robinson Leary's hair had gone from salt and pepper to almost all white in the nine years she had been at Meadow Lakes. She was slender and almost as tall as Hadley. Her husband had died spooned in her arms in their bed in their Old Market apartment. Both had been professors at Creighton University, and Robbie had needed a change right after his death. She retired early and moved to the retirement community where she had found Table 12.

She also found a short romance with an Apache named Raven. He was big, strong, tall, handsome and intelligent. Like Janet Evanovich's "Ranger" character, he owned a security company, but Raven made Ranger look like a short wimp. A pro football player when Alphonso Greatwood, a Kansas City Chief's linebacker was in the game, he had been called in by his old football buddy when Meadow

Lakes had fallen victim to Dr. Fell. Robbie thought about all that now and then.

She thought a lot more about Raven…a lot more.

Her skin was the shade of a rich latte and she claimed both African-American heritage and a little Cajun as well. By the time spring peeked its head through the trees at Meadow Lakes, she was going to find out a lot more about her heritage, whether she wanted to or not, because your past is always with you. You can bury it but it digs its way out and comes back with teeth a-snapping to bite you in the ass unless you honor and accept it and make the changes it requires.

Marge Aaron, like Mary Rose McGill, decided a short nap was in order after the wine and cheese. She went into her apartment, leaned back in her recliner and turned on the golf channel. She didn't play golf, didn't like golf and thought those little white balls were only there to ruin a perfectly good walk. But the golf channel was guaranteed to put her to sleep. She had once asked why a nap like this was called "beauty sleep" when you wake up looking like a troll. But naps were good and Marge, along with Mary Rose, believed that at her age, they were mandatory.

"Marge Aaron - say it fast and it's Margarine," she had told the other three friends when they first met.

She had come to Meadow Lakes on contract with the Omaha Police Department to solve the murder of one Percolator Rasmussen. The back of Perky's head had been smashed in, his throat cut and with a nylon cord around his neck, a bullet hole in his jacket and a knife in his back. It didn't take Marge long to figure out this was probably not a suicide.

Marge was a large lady who should be large. She would have looked strange thin and petite. She liked to say that a recent study showed that women who were somewhat overweight lived longer than men who mentioned it. Her knees were bad (one had been replaced) and she was stiff as a rail when she got up in the morning. "Old age is coming at a really bad time," she said now and then.

She had been a good cop, solved some bad murders and put away some bad guys. Her colleagues had respected her and she was proud of that and proud that she had married law enforcement and given birth to law enforcement. Her husband was a "cop's cop" and her children were police and FBI.

The Red Cane

Marge's prize procession was a lethal weapon, a red cane, shiny and bright. It was usually at home hung casually over the back of whatever chair was holding her ample behind.

The cane actually seemed to have a personality of its own and it had "bling." Push one jewel and it turned into a taser, another and it was a low-powered rifle, a third jewel sent tripping pellets all over the floor and a fourth produced a huge smoke screen.

The final jewel shot knives out the sides and there was a golden lariat in the handle, just like Wonder Woman's. Wonder Woman was such a comic book superhero.

Marge loved her red cane and for that matter, so did the other BOOB Girls. It tended to come in handy now and then.

The BOOB Girls: warrior women of justice!

Their motto was Never Underestimate A Burned Out Old Broad.

The Men in the Story

Alphonso Greatwood and Wiley Vondra were close friends. While the girls believed that women have a different friendship gene than men - making friends quicker, keeping them longer and having more, these two men were like brothers who liked each other.

Alphonso Greatwood. A big black man, Alphonso had been a lineman for the Kansas City Chiefs when the club really got underway in the 1960's. He was still huge. Even though he wasn't terribly overweight, his big frame and his still-strong muscles had added to the body stress caused by the many hits he took on the field and his knees were shot beyond repair.

Both his knees and Marge's looked as if they had lost a head-butting contest with midgets.

Alphonso Greatwood was pretty well scooter-bound. But his scooter was custom made and outstanding. The Green Machine was, of course, painted green. It had a detachable roll bar and a GPS. When Alphonso pushed one button, it played the Nebraska fight song. A second button rendered the theme song from the old television show; "Happy Days," because Alphonso Greatwood was the original "Fonz." There was a seat behind the driver's that had "Bitch Seat" written on it.

Last year, when he began to gently and tenderly court Marge Aaron, he had painted the seat yellow, realized the whole scooter looked like it belonged to a Green Bay Packer, and he had repainted it the same green shade as the rest of The Green Machine.

Good move.

Alphonso basked in his notoriety. He was still interviewed by sports writers. The sports broadcast team of Mike and Mike called him now and then for a commentary. When Raven was at Meadow Lakes, the two old pros still made an impressive entrance into the dining room.

He also basked in his love for Meadow Lakes Reluctant to move there because a retirement community meant he was growing old, he came to love the place so much he bought it from the wicked Busch family from Florida.

Thorney, Lilac and Rose Busch had turned it into a den of iniquity with liquor, gambling, prostitution and an underground Viagra ring.

Alphonso was a good owner. Sheryl, his manager was good, too and together they made the place a showroom for modern retirement living and luxury.

Wiley Vondra, a little older than Alphonso, was tall and lanky. A cowboy at one time in western

Nebraska, he was always seen in cowboy boots, a brown leather vest and a Stetson hat. While each apartment had a washer and dryer, on the 15th of every month, hat, vest and boots were all Wiley wore when he did his laundry in the old Meadow Lakes laundry room. The girls had met him there when Maggie Patten threw open the door to the laundry room, found Wiley at a card table with a hand of solitaire and Willie Nelson wailing on a boom box.

 "Hello, Ladies!" he had grinned. "You want a game of poker?" Now, he and Mary Rose were an item and had cared deeply for each other for eight years.

Wiley was a Korean War veteran, "The Forgotten War," he called it, and he still, now and then on certain dates, wept in the shower. On other days, the song that was played over and over for the troops ran through Wiley's head and he would softly sing aloud, "Rag Mopp, dodily do de ah dah. Rag Mopp, diddily do de oohdo, R-a-g-g-m-o-p-p-Ragg Mop!." He often sang it all the way down the long hall as he went to his apartment.

Wiley had never married after he returned from the war, had no children or pets. But he had Mary Rose McGill and considered himself a lucky man.

A very lucky man indeed.

Purple Snowmobiles and Rats

The girls each had a pair of binoculars pressed against their eyebrows and cheeks. They were standing at the big dining room windows staring out into the whiteness. A huge flock of tiny winter juncos was eating birdseed thrown out for them, chattering away and entertaining the residents of Meadow Lakes.

"I love them," Mary Rose said. "They look like little nuns."

The girls nodded. The birds made everyone happy, and there were so many of them. It was the biggest flock any of them had seen and usually, you only saw them a few at a time.

The girls were watching so intently that it took a minute to realize they were hearing a motor coming closer and closer. They lowered their binoculars and looked around over the drifts.

"There," Marge said, pointing toward the far end of the big lawn. The binoculars shot back to their eyes.

"Holy Moly," Hadley said.

"Wow!" Mary Rose exclaimed.

Robbie added a, "What is it?"

"Who is it, is more likely," Marge answered.

They were glued to the sight roaring across the snow.

A purple snowmobile was bouncing high into the air with every drift. Standing, with knees bent, hands on the wheel, was a tall figure in a purple snowsuit.

A purple stocking cap with a gigantic tassel flew behind the figure's head. As the snowmobile rapidly approached and turned to avoid a fallen branch, they could see a small cage securely strapped behind the driver.

"What's in there?" Robbie asked.

"It looks like tiny little animals in sweaters," Mary Rose said, leaning forward, binoculars pressed to her eyes.

"I can't tell," Hadley said.

"Rats!" Marge said.

Mary Rose took her glasses from her face and looked at Marge, "It's all right, Marge, we'll see them when they get closer, for Heaven's sake."

"No," Marge said. "Rats. The little animals in the cage wearing those tiny sweaters are white rats."

"Oh," the other three said together.

The snowmobile careened and twisted past the dining room, sending a huge spray of snow against the window where the girls were standing. They instinctively took a step back.

"That was a woman," Hadley said.

"A very tall woman," Robbie observed.

"With rats," Mary Rose added.

"Headed for the front door," Marge said.

They were quiet. In just a few minutes they heard the sound of the automatic front door sliding open. Footsteps sounded down the hall toward Alphonso's office.

Marge turned to her friends. "We're not missing this!"

They hurried toward the dining room doors and the long hallway to Alphonso's office, binoculars swinging from their necks. When they were just a few steps into the hall Mary Rose McGill said, loudly, "SHIT!"

It wasn't the usual expletive. It meant "Shoulders back, Head high, Eyes (I's) straight ahead and Tummy tucked in. Even though they were walking as fast as they could for old ladies, they straightened up and had remarkably good posture.

Chaos Cauldron

They came to a sudden stop just outside Alphonso's office door. Laughter drifted through the heavy wood; deep laughter from Alphonso and a bell-like tinkle from a female voice. They heard the female voice say, "Darn!" and laugh beautifully. Alphonso's deep laugh joined hers.

Marge knocked three times and opened the door without hearing a "come in" or "enter" from Alphonso. He looked over at them from his desk, smiled, then put a hand out, palm up, toward the tall woman standing before him.

"BOOB Girls, meet my old friend, Chaos Cauldron." He was smiling from ear to ear.

Chaos Cauldron was tall all right, very tall. In her snow boots, she must have been at least six feet, two inches. Even through the bulky purple snowsuit, the girls could tell she was pencil thin.

I don't think I like her, Hadley thought, eyeing her trim figure.

Chaos' hair was short, snow white and spiked. Some of the spikes were lying against her head, pushed down from her heavy cap. As the girls came inside Alphonso's office, Chaos unzipped the snowsuit and began to step out of it. She was wearing a black T-shirt with "I Kill Zombies" written in white with red blood splashes surrounding it.

A Fashionista

As her long, black-leggings-clad legs came out of the suit, she reached one arm around to pick it up.

Running entirely up her arm was a bright, colorful tattoo of an enormous snake. It was clear the snake had only one eye.

Robinson Leary gasped. Her hand shot to her mouth, and then shot back down to her side almost instantly. She stared intently at Chaos' arm. "Zombi," she whispered to herself.

"Hi," Chaos said. "Pleased to meet you all." She had a soft, mellow New Orleans tang in her voice. She folded the snowsuit and started moving Alphonso's office chairs close to his desk as an invitation for the girls to sit down.

They sat.

Before she took her seat, Chaos walked to beside Alphonso's desk, bent toward the floor and picked up the cage they had seen earlier. Three big, fat, white rats caught their balance and hung on as she swung the cage around for the girls to see.

"Meet my familiars," Chaos smiled a warm but somewhat wicked smile. She pointed to the three rats who were wearing tiny variegated sweaters knit with very thin, but warm, yarn. Chaos reached into the cage and picked up one rat by the tail. The girls winced. "Double-Double," Chaos said, pointing to the rat. She dropped the rat and picked up the second one, again by the tail. "Toil," was the second rat's name and the last one picked up was called, "Trouble."

"The three witches from Macbeth," Robbie said softly. She was still glancing furtively at the snake that appeared to slither up the arm of Ms. Cauldron.

"Right!" Chaos said, "Double-Double, Toil and Trouble." She dropped the third rat back into the cage.

"Chaos is from New Orleans," Alphonso said, still smiling. "She's a voodoo queen in training."

They looked at her and then at Alphonso, who was thoroughly enjoying the moment.

"How do you two know each other?" Marge asked, her voice a little tight.

"The Chiefs played football in New Orleans," Alphonso answered. "Chaos practiced her spells on the opposition."

"Never liked the New Orleans Saints," Chaos said, her voice low, "Couldn't win then, can't win now. Darn! You know the old saying, 'It's not over till the fat lady sings?' Well, a couple of times they were so bad the fat lady sang the National Anthem."

"Did the spells work?" Mary Rose asked, her eyes wide.

"Yep," Chaos said. "They always lost when Alphonso was on the field."

Alphonso grinned wider. "They lost when I wasn't on the field, too."

"But remember," Chaos said, looking at the girls who were seated in the chairs watching her like a bird watches a worm, "I'm only in training. I can't make Love Potion Number Nine. I'm only on Six."

"What are you doing here?" Robbie asked. Her eyes finally left the snake and looked at Chaos' face. It was a very attractive face covered with very small wrinkles. She appeared to be about the same age as the girls.

"Wanted to see the man here," Chaos said, looking at Alphonso.

Marge shifted uncomfortably in her chair. "You said the rats were your familiars. I thought only witches had familiars." Marge had already decided she didn't like this thin woman either.

"Darn! Familiar, Samiliar," Chaos shrugged. "If you love a rat, you can call it anything you want."

Robbie turned to Hadley. "I've known some men like that," she said softly.

Chaos opened the cage door again and the three rats jumped onto her shoulders and sat looking at the girls. It was a strange sight.

"Oh my god," Hadley said, leaning back as if the rats might jump from Chaos to her shoulder.

"Sweet Jesus," Robbie chimed in.

"Jesus, Mary and Joseph," Mary Rose added, still smiling a little smile.

Marge joined the religious litany of rat watchers. "Holy shit!"

Mary Rose, the animal lover, smiled in spite of herself.

"Darn! I hate witches," Chaos continued, the rats snuggled into her shirt. "They don't do real spells and they've gotten way too much publicity. I say, 'May the powers of the universe reign and assault them.'"

Mary Rose leaned toward Robbie and whispered, "Did she just ask somebody to rain salt on witches?"

Robbie thought for a second, then leaned back toward Mary Rose without looking at her. "Close enough, girlfriend," she whispered back.

Falling for You

Alphonso reached into his desk, took out a key on a small chain and dangled it so Chaos could see it. "Chaos will be in the guest suite on your floor for a few weeks," he said, smiling toward the girls.

Chaos reached out, took the key and with the other hand opened the little cage. The rats scrambled down her arm and jumped into the cage. They turned toward their mistress, their bright eyes watching her. Chaos grabbed her snow suit, raised one long-fingered hand toward the girls, gave them a little finger wave, smiled and said, "Toodle."

"Toodle?" Hadley asked as Alphonso's door closed behind Chaos. "As in toodle-oo?"

"British," Robbie mumbled, "a traveler's farewell when embarking on a long walk."

They looked at her.

She looked troubled.

"I know that snake," she said, shaking her head. "I know that snake." Then she stood, shrugged, grinned and headed toward the door, followed by Hadley and Mary Rose.

"Catch you later," Marge called after them. "I want to see 'the man' here." She did a good imitation of Chaos' voice.

She walked over and stood beside Alphonso, who leaned back in his expensive leather desk chair. Marge tried to keep the whine out of her voice and was mostly successful.

"Who is she, Alphonso, and even more, who is she to you?"

"She's not even a friend," Alphonso answered. "A football groupie from the old days and who she is to me is just that. We never had a date, we never had a drink together, but I always felt kind of sorry for her. Nothing seems to go right for her and believe me, she wouldn't know voodoo from Who Do?" He shook his head.

"I heard in recent years she pretty much wanders around the country doing what she calls 'training and research.'"

Marge and Alphonso dated off and on. Their only kisses had been pecks on the cheek and Marge was surprised that what she was feeling was a close cousin to jealousy. "OK," she said, feeling embarrassed, "just wondered."

She started to turn toward the door, red cane over her arm, when Alphonso grabbed her hand. She turned and looked at him, and then he did something totally unexpected. He turned his chair toward her and patted his lap.

"Sit down, lady," he said softly.

Marge looked at him, then at his lap, then, with a delicate move for a large lady, she gently sat on the big man's lap.

He turned her face toward him to kiss her on the lips.

First, they heard the tall, adjustable base of the over-priced chair crack loudly. Then they heard the four wheels splay flat out, then they heard their own laughter as they fell on top of each other onto the floor.

A loud crash echoed through the big office as four hundred pounds of human beings and the big chair hit the floor.

Alphonso laughed a deep, hearty laugh and then turned toward Marge whose sweat shirt had pulled up, showing her bra, and whose face was slowly turning red.

Alphonso looked at that face, smiled, turned toward her and gave her a sweet, gentle kiss on the lips.

Marge kissed him back.

Way to go.

Pillow Talk

The weather finally broke. The sun came out; the snow began to settle in, then began to melt. Things began to look normal.

A new lady on the scene, in addition to Chaos, was Julie, who came in to make Meadow Lakes even more attractive. A florist by trade and desire, Julie was outdoorsy, comfortable and attractive. She wore sweatshirts and sweatpants, sneakers and a fun garden hat, even indoors. She kept the plants up to snuff, arranged flowers in every area and thoroughly enjoyed her job.

It was Julie who discovered the pillows.

"Those are, without a doubt, the ugliest pillows I've ever seen," Hadley said. They were looking at two chairs in the main lobby that had just been brought in and, interestingly enough, no one, including Alphonso, seemed to know where they had come from.

One was a bright paisley with red, blue and yellow colors. The other had a busy Victorian pattern that clashed with its partner chair, the paisley. But the real clash, the eye-injuring sight that came into view when anyone looked at the two chairs, was the pillows.

A paisley pillow perfectly matched the paisley chair.

The Victorian patterned pillow was at home in the Victorian chair.

But when the pillows were switched around, the effect was catastrophic.

Ugly.

Terrible.

When they were switched and he first saw them Geoffrey lay down, put his head on the floor and covered his eyes with his big, long front legs.

And dogs are supposed to be color blind!

"They can't even sing," Hadley said.

They looked at her. Robbie did an eyeroll.

"There was this Italian opera singer who was the best in the world," Hadley said, grinning widely. "But he was so ugly (she pronounced it "oogly") that people covered their heads with sacks when he sang. But this one woman loved his voice, followed him to every concert and finally married him.

They went to his village to live and the first time the bride went to the market, another woman came up to her and said, "You are zee bride."

"I yam," the bride said.

"I must ask you," the woman said, "He eez so oogly. How do you sleep with him?"

The bride shook her head. "Eet eez not easy," she said. "Sometimes in the night I wake up and I shove him in zee arm." She demonstrated by pushing Mary Rose's arm twice. "And I say, 'Wake up! Sing! Sing!'"

"Those pillows can't even sing." Hadley was proud of her joke. The other girls were proud to roll their eyes again.

"They seem to change on their own," Julie said. "I can walk by and they're where they should be. Then five minutes later, they're changed and no one has been here."

Julie was holding a small little box that seemed to wiggle now and then. She looked at the box. "What's just as strange, this morning, I found this in one of the big flower pots by the elevator."

She moved toward them and they gathered around the box. Julie opened it and they looked at a tiny little garden snake, wiggling and squirming frantically on the cardboard bottom.

"Yuk," Mary Rose said, and they all, except Marge and Geoffrey, took a step back.

"It's just a baby," Marge said. She looked at Julie. "Put her in the compost pile, Julie. It's warm there and she'll make it until spring comes." Marge got a wicked smile on her face that included her twinkly eyes. "Maybe she'll get big enough to eat rats." The girls rolled their eyes one more time.

Normal is Nice

As the snow melted and Thanksgiving approached, Chaos became a regular presence at Table 12. She would pull up her chair and make herself at home. "There's always room for one more at Table 12," Mary Rose said – over and over.

Chaos was pleasant. They actually enjoyed her. Her warped mind, strange sense of humor and her off-the-wall beliefs fascinated them. She really did want to be a voodoo queen, and they all gave her points for trying. So far no evidence of "voodoo-ness" had appeared.

"Did you put a spell on the pillows in the ugly chairs?" Hadley joked one day. The pillows had been hopping back and forth, driving Julie into a frenzy. Chaos just smiled.

Any spell Chaos would put on the pillows probably involved using both hands.

And she was wrapped up in how her past was important, just as Willie Winkie had been the year before.

"We don't realize that our past is our roots," Chaos would say. "Our ancestors, rest their souls, had a part in making us who we are. We ARE our past. We grow from it like we grow our own souls."

"Now you're a theologian," Robbie said with a smile.

Chaos just nodded, "Darn right!"

Just three days after she arrived, the first day delivery trucks could plow through the snow, six big boxes arrived for her.

"Clothes and makeup?" Hadley asked.

"Potions and lotions?" Robbie suggested.

"Horridly scary things and spices for spells?" Mary Rose added.

"Probably ordered online," Hadley said. "Hard to get those things from Hy-Vee."

"Or Mangelsen's," Mary Rose said.

"Never seen them at Trader Joe's," Robbie smiled.

"Rats!" Marge said.

"No way!" The other three said together.

Chaos spent most of her time in the guest suite. They had never been invited in.

"It's OK. I don't go where rats live," Mary Rose had said.

"She seems nice enough," Robbie added, "just somehow strangely lonely."

"She wants my red cane," Marge said. "She looks at it like she's willing it to follow her home. The other day she rubbed it before she handed it to me."

Hadley laughed. "I told her maybe she could cast a spell on it so it would hop along behind you wherever you go like the brooms in *The Sorcerer's Apprentice*."

"Maybe she can make it like the magic wands in *Harry Potter*," Robbie added. "It could leap into the air whenever you hold out your hand."

"Maybe she'll turn it into a broom and you can fly on it, proving to us all you really can drive a stick."

They all looked at Mary Rose.

"That was funny!" Hadley said.

They nodded – all except Marge.

The first surprise came when Chaos came to Table 12 with a small, beautiful box, like the ones that hold jewelry. She sat the box on the table, pulled up a chair and grinned.

"I have a new familiar," she said, still smiling.

She opened the box.

Inside, curled up warm and cozy in a comfortable nest of fake grass, was - - - the little garden snake.

Spell #1: Cane it be True?

There was still snow on the ground, so only the extremely brave and foolish took walks outside.

Mary Rose had encouraged exercise by, with Wiley's help, creating a map, where they could walk each day, record how far they walked and by Christmas, would have walked far enough to get to Bethlehem. Everyone at Meadow Lakes was interested and became involved. Sometimes at mid-day the halls would be full of people walking and talking and laughing. It had turned into a good idea.

"We'll be lucky to walk far enough to get to Council Bluffs, Iowa" Hadley had joked as she puffed down the hall to keep up with Robbie.

"Maybe Gretna, Nebraska." Robbie had wheezed back

But this day, Marge was out before sunrise. Her knee was bothering her and she was using the old sports solution, "Walk it off!" She was doing her best, but she was using the red cane like a regular cane. It marched along beside her - step, clump, step, clump. And the pain was getting better when Marge heard a little "ping."

She thought nothing of it.

"Ping."

"Ping."

She looked around. Nothing.

"Clunk."

The cane vibrated in her hand.

She looked down.

Attached to her cane were at least ten paper clips of different shapes and sizes. As she watched, a piece of an old watch sailed through the air and, with a "bing" attached itself to the cane. A quilting needle seemed to jump up from the thick carpet to find a place near the bottom.

Marge brought the cane up to eye level and looked at it. Her eyes opened wide. "It looks pitiful," she said aloud.

Before she finished her sentence, a small stapler flew through the air and smacked against the back of the cane with such force that Marge took a step backward.

"Chaos?" She whispered.

Marge remembered how, as she had told the girls, after dinner one night, Chaos had gotten up quickly, walked to Marge's cane and picked it up, as if to hand it to the detective. Marge remembered that, as Chaos handed it to her, she had smiled and rubbed her hand along the back of the cane, as if she were putting lotion on an outstretched arm. She was mumbling something under her breath.

"Chaos!" Marge repeated loudly. And she said it even as she didn't believe for a minute in voodoo or spells or anything like that. Marge Aaron was nothing if not tough and practical.

She turned down the hall and hurried toward the dining room, the cane heavier due to all the metal attached to it.

She was hurrying as fast as she could, and as she went by the hall to the lobby, she didn't notice that, once again, the pillows were in the wrong chairs.

As she passed the elevators, there was a crash behind her. A picture had fallen from the wall and the metal hook that had held it zoomed toward the cane and attached itself with a loud "Bang!"

In front of the dining room, three spoons and an evil looking steak knife shot through the doors and landed between the smoke screen jewel and the rifle.

By the time Marge got to Table 12, the cane was covered with metal debris.

Dawn was just breaking over the snow. Marge could hear the staff laughing in the kitchen but, as for the dining room, Marge Aaron, homicide detective, was totally alone and totally confused and worried. For the first time in a long time, she felt like crying.

In only a few minutes residents started filing in for breakfast. Marge saw Geoffrey come to the door, lie down in his usual spot with the, "I'm not allowed in there when people food is being served," pitiful look and Marge knew Mary Rose would be first to reach Table 12.

"Hey, Marge," she smiled.

"Hey back and look at this!"

Marge held up the metal-covered cane which did, indeed, look as if it felt sorry for itself.

"Marge, that doesn't look good." Mary Rose said. "I hate to tell you this but it's not a good decorating idea."

"I didn't do it!"

Robbie joined them and was standing alongside Mary Rose.

"Yuk," was all she said, frowning at the strange-looking cane.

Hadley came up to stand with them. As she stood there, a pair of tiny, antique sewing scissors flew out of a resident's pocket and lit gracefully on the side of the cane, just under the taser jewel.

Marge held the cane out to Hadley.

"Put 'em back, will you?"

Hadley reached down, pulled the little scissors off and headed back toward their owner.

"What's happening?" Hadley asked, staring at the cursed cane. "If you didn't do this, who did?"

"Chaos Cauldron!" Marge yelled, standing up.

Chaos was striding through the door wearing black jeans and a black sweatshirt with a picture of a snake on the font.

Chaos hurried to the table, took one look at the cane and said, "Darn!"

"Darn?" Marge said a little too loudly. People near them were beginning to watch and Wiley Vondra was hurrying through the dining room doors. "Is that all you have to say?"

There was total quiet. Other diners soon ignored them and started their own table conversations.

"Chaos," Robbie said in a friendly but firm voice. "Did you put a spell on the red cane?"

Chaos looked confused.

"I guess so," she finally said. They looked at her. There was a good two minutes of silence.

Marge was still glaring, then all at once she said, "Everyone sit down."

They sat.

They looked at the voodoo queen in training.

Chaos smiled a weak smile. "I did," she finally said, "but not that one."

Marge frowned. The others sat with their mouths slightly open.

"I liked Hadley's idea of it following you like in *The Sorcerer's Apprentice*." She sighed a little sigh. "So I mixed up a potion – it smelled really good – but I must have done something wrong. What I did turned into…." She looked at the cane which was lying in the middle of the table, still covered with small metal objects.

"A magnetic spell," Mary Rose said. It looked as if she was ready to clap her hands until Marge glared at her.

They were quiet again.

"Darn! I'm sorry, Marge," Chaos said softly. "I won't touch your cane again." She looked as if she were the one ready to cry.

Marge showed no sympathy. "Take it all off."

Chaos held out her arms, her palms up, gave a helpless look and shrugged.

Marge stood up and banged the tip of the cane on the table. All the objects clattered and pinged themselves off.

"That's part of my problem," Chaos said, looking around at them. "My spells don't have much hang time."

They began picking up small objects and putting them in separate stacks.

"Ooh," Chaos said, holding up four bobby pins, "who uses bobby pins anymore?"

They all looked at Mary Rose who held out her hand to take the bobby pins.

"One thing, Marge," Mary Rose said, pocketing the bobby pins. "You're going to have enough paper clips to last for years."

For the first time that morning, Marge Aaron smiled.

Old Women are Tigers

"That is way too much action for me," Marge said as they walked down the hall after breakfast. Her knee still hurt and she was using the cane and limping a little. "And I'm a retired homicide detective!"

Geoffrey walked behind them. He would have liked to have trotted, but trotting with these women was out of the question. He kept up the slow pace.

Good dog.

"I'm sorry," Chaos said for the umpteenth time.

As they rounded the first turn toward Hadley's apartment, they saw a young man working on one of the water fountains near the lobby rest rooms. He was overweight, had greasy-looking hair and when bending over, his jeans were showing a butt crack just slightly smaller than the Grand Canyon.

"Why do they do that?" Robbie asked, shaking her head. "Don't they know they look stupid?"

"Only to us oldsters," Hadley said.

Then he turned around and they saw the writing on the front of his T-shirt.

They stopped.

"Oh my God!" Robbie said.

"Sweet Jesus," Mary Rose said.

Hadley squinted. "What does it say? I can't see it."

Chaos started to tell her. "It says, 'Women are Cun-'"
And Mary Rose clapped her hand over Chaos' mouth.

"Well," Marge said, "It's C-U-N and it's NOT
'Cunning.' Then it says. "Men Rule. Show the
bitches."

"That's awful! Hadley said, and without warning,
she walked to the nearest table, picked up a candle
holder, carefully removed the candle and walked
toward the young man with the derogatory shirt.

"Yo, Old Woman," the kid said.

"Yo, back," Hadley replied and she raised the candle
stick and hit him as hard as she could upside the
head.

"Ow! What the hell you think you're…"

But before he could finish, Mary Rose wound up with
the famous groin kick she had perfected in Book II,
took a powerful kick and dislocated his knee.

"Ow! Bitches!"

"No," Robbie said, "we're tigers. We're women. We're tough and we don't like your taste in clothes."

Geoffrey saw a great chance to play. Sometimes his ladies were really fun. He backed up, took aim, ran toward the kid, jumped on his chest and knocked him flat.

"Ow! Damn dog!"

Geoffrey grabbed the tail of his shirt. The cheap shirt started to rip. The more it ripped, the harder Geoffrey pulled. And with that, Robbie bent over the man, put her hand through a hole in the shirt and began to tear it off of him, working along with the big mastiff.

Hadley was beating him with two candlesticks now. Mary Rose was kicking his legs and he looked like he was trying to dance the Turkey Trot lying down. Robbie and Geoffrey kept ripping until the most of the shirt came off in her hands. Geoffrey was adding to the excitement with deep growls and shaking his head with another piece of the shirt in his mouth. The shirt was almost off. Chaos had her hands in prayer position and was mumbling loudly, her voice blending in with Geoffrey's growls.

The young man was saying, "Damn it! Quit it!" Over and over.

Mary Rose McGill was saying, "Never underestimate a burned out old broad," over and over.

He squirmed and wiggled and dodged until he was on his feet – unsteady, but upright. His hands were trying to grab the candlesticks but Geoffrey was too much of a snarling, snapping distraction.

"We are nasty women!" Mary Rose yelled. "And nasty women are tigers!"

Marge looked at the scene before her and sighed. "This is ridiculous."

She walked behind the young man, who was getting steadier on his feet and ready to fight back. She raised her cane and tasered him in the balls.

He went down with a crash.

Geoffrey jumped sideways to get out of the way. Smart dog.

The girls looked at each other. Everyone except Marge and Chaos was puffing at the exercise.

Chaos walked slowly over to the fallen creep, took

a small vial out of her jeans pocket and poured the contents into his ear.

"What's that?" Robbie asked.

"A potion that will make dandelions grow out of wherever you pour it."

"Why didn't you pour it on his crotch?" Hadley asked.

Chaos shrugged, "Darn! Didn't think of it."

A crowd had gathered and was applauding.

"It takes very little to amuse old people," Marge mumbled.

The crowd parted and Alphonso came through on the Green Machine. Wiley was puffing and panting beside him.

Alphonso just looked at the girls, his eyebrows raised. Robbie showed him the shirt which still had the lettering intact. His eyebrows held an additional conversation with his receding hairline.

"We don't like him," Mary Rose said.

"And soo, dandelions will sprout out of his ear," Chaos added.

The young man was starting to get up, shaky, but fairly well balanced. He looked around through blurry eyes.

"You're beautiful," he said, looking at Marge. "Will you go out with me?"

He looked at Hadley. "And you are just gorgeous, my dear. Please let me be your knight in shining armor."

Then he looked at Alphonso. "Oh wonderful sir, I think I love you."

"Darn!" Chaos said. "I did it wrong. I made Love Potion Number Four. At this rate I'll never get to Love Potion Number Nine." She shook her head. "Darn! I hope I wrote down what I put in it." And she turned around and hurried down the hall toward her suite.

Alphonso looked at the young man who was gazing into the big man's eyes with a puppy dog look. "Out!" Alphonso said. "Now!"

The young man began to weep, picked up his tools and staggered out the front door. As far as they could tell, he was still crying.

Wiley walked to Mary Rose. "Mary Rose McGill, you've got to stop doing things like this!"

Mary Rose put her hands on her hips and scowled at him. "Wiley Vondra, we've been through a lot together these last nine years and most of it was your fault!"

She turned and hurried down the hall, Wiley right behind her, arms outstretched as if he were explaining something.

Hadley, Robbie and Marge headed toward the lobby.

"Does this mean we're feminists?" Hadley asked.

"All old women are feminists," Robbie said. "Some are activists, some deny it, some just believe women are equal to men, but we're all Momma Tigers under the skin."

"You know that little voice inside your head that tells you not to do something you shouldn't do?" Marge asked, striding forward and not turning toward them.

They nodded.

"BOOB Girls don't have that."

Hadley looked at the two chairs in the lobby as they went past. The pillows were on the wrong chairs again.

She walked over and switched them.

"Julie did a really good job on those planters," she said, as if it was just another normal morning in Meadow Lakes land. The big planters in the lobby were rich with fall flowers. Marge limped along beside them. "Like I said before, I've had enough action for one day."

But that's when the real action began.

Witchy-Witchy-Woo

The snow started again the day before Thanksgiving. Alphonso, being a good weather watcher, had ordered enough food for two holidays. He was wise. The roads were once again blocked and, while city crews did a good job clearing the main thoroughfare, the snow prevented most family members from getting to the retirement community to enjoy Thanksgiving dinner.

The Thanksgiving feast was excellent and – again, it was Mary Rose's idea – there was enough turkey left for the residents to take to their apartments, cook and present a "Cluck and Gobble" leftover turkey casserole cook-off. (See the back of this book for the winners.)

The day after the feast, all but Chaos vowing to lose weight, they stood at the big windows of the dining room looking once more over the drifts that covered the lawns.

"It's vicious, but beautiful," Hadley said.

"Snow on snow on snow," Robbie repeated.

"Makes my knee ache," Marge added.

Mary Rose moved a step closer to the window and

pointed. "Look! Someone has stuck a cute little barber pole in the snow."

They all moved closer and squinted. "I don't see it," Hadley said.

They looked harder at where Mary Rose pointed.

"Oh, no!" Marge said. She turned and hurried down the hall toward her apartment.

"She doesn't like barber poles?" Mary Rose asked.

Marge came limping back in just minutes, her binoculars in her hand. She hurried to the window, leaned her cane against the glass and stared through the binoculars.

"It's not a barber pole," she said, without turning toward them. "It's a human leg sticking up into the air. And it has a red and white striped stocking with a black dress boot, just like in the pictures you see of witches." She pulled out her phone to dial 911.

Hadley, Robbie and Mary Rose looked at her with their mouths slightly open.

Behind them, Chaos Cauldron dropped somewhat gracefully to the floor in a faint.

They all turned and looked at her.

No one moved to pick her up.

Mary Rose shook her head. "I thought voodoo was a vengeful, dark art with dolls that had pins sticking in them. But I like Chaos."

Finally, Robbie moved to lift Chaos's head. "I think Chaos is doomed to a kinder, gentler kind of voodoo."

"Don't mention dolls and pins to her, Mary Rose," Hadley advised.

Chaos opened her eyes.

"Darn!" She said.

Ron the Cop

In what seemed like hours, a path was plowed from the back door of Meadow Lake's far wing to the crime scene. Yellow tape surrounded a generous area around the body. Men and women in Omaha Police Department and Crime Scene uniforms were carefully digging and scraping snow from around the corpse, being careful not to destroy or mishandle evidence. A huge Med Tech van stood by, its motor running and pouring white exhaust into the air. As they watched, an unmarked police car literally skidded to a stop outside the tape. A well-built man, in black slacks and a red, white and blue leather jacket stepped out.

"Why is it," Robbie mused, looking at the jacket, "we all love the colors red, white and blue unless they're flashing behind us?"

Every window at Meadow Lakes was filled with the faces of residents watching the action. The boring times of winter were apparently ending.

"OMG!" Marge said, louder than she intended. She stared again through the binoculars, "I think - - yep, I know – that is Ron the Cop." She gave a little giggle and clapped her hands while still holding the binoculars.

That was very unlike Marge Aaron.

The girls squinted at the figure in the red, white and blue jacket. He was of medium height, had brown, sandy hair and, while they couldn't see them, he had some of the brightest blue eyes imaginable. He had a straight, military posture and it was easy to picture him on a motorcycle when the weather warmed up.

Marge headed back toward her apartment. Chaos was standing, still weak, at the window with them now.

"Darn!" She kept whispering over and over. They weren't paying attention to her.

As they watched, in just a few minutes Marge appeared, exiting the far back door. She had on her heavy winter coat and snow boots and she was hurrying along the path to the crime scene, leaning on her red cane.

They saw Ron the Cop turn toward her; put his hand over his forehead to shade his eyes, wait for a few seconds, then quickly climb over the yellow tape and hurry toward Marge, who was making pretty good progress toward him.

"Marge?" Ron said, his arms spread wide.

"Ron!" Marge replied.

He folded her into a huge bear hug and the girls were sure, if he could have, he would have lifted the retired detective off the ground and spun around with her.

While they couldn't hear the two law enforcement officers, they could tell what was going on.

"What have you got, Ron?" Marge asked, pointing at the red and white stocking still sticking into the air.

"Looks like a murdered woman in a witch costume."

Marge moved in and leaned over the body. It was an older lady, her face painted witch green, dressed totally as a Halloween witch with long black dress, black pointed hat, red and white stockings and black boots. One stocking and boot had been removed and Marge immediately knew where it was. What the girls had thought was a leg sticking up in the air was actually a broom holding a cardboard cylinder covered with the stocking and boot.

"Like a marker or a sign post," Marge said to Ron, pointing to the broom leg.

"We've also got an ID on her," Ron said. "It was in her pocket." He looked down at a plastic bag holding several small cards and a few dollars. "Winifred Wyttch."

"Winifred Witch?" Marge asked.

"Spelled W-y-t-t-c-h."

Marge almost smiled thinking of how Robbie would roll her eyes at that name.

They talked quietly while looking at poor Winifred's stiff, still and obviously dead body.

Meanwhile, back at the window, Hadley, Robbie and Mary Rose had gotten their binoculars and were watching Marge and Ron the Cop.

Chaos was sitting in one of the big easy chairs repeating, "Darn," like a mantra.

Geoffrey had appeared and was doing an Olympic doggie sit beside the girls, looking out the window with them. The only difference was that he was watching for rabbits not humans. Every so often he turned and looked quickly at Chaos and her mumblings.

He liked Chaos.

She smelled like rats.

"What's going on?" Julie, the decorator, came up beside them carrying snowshoes and wearing a snowsuit with shiny black boots and a bright orange hat.

"There's a body in the snow," Mary Rose told her. "A dead one."

"A lot of that going around these days," Julie replied. "What happened?"

"We don't know yet," Hadley answered, still looking out the window, "but Marge is out there and now it looks as if she's starting back inside"

Marge had given Ron the Cop another hug, turned and begun a slow walk toward the far back door.

"While I think of it," Julie said, "are any of you switching the pillows in the two chairs in the lobby?"

They looked at her. She shrugged.

It took Marge several minutes to reach the window in the dining room. "Murdered woman in a witch's costume," she said. "That's not a real leg. It's cardboard with a stocking and boot. Like it's there to mark where she lay." Marge shook her head.

"Do we know who she is…was?" Mary Rose said.

Marge looked at Robbie. "Her name is Winifred Wyttch. And that's spelled, W-y-t-t-c-h."

As expected, Robbie did an eyeroll and said, "Winifred Witch? Spelled W-y-t-t-c-h? You've got to be kidding!" She did a second eyeroll.

"Darn!" Chaos said again.

Julie moved toward the window to get a better look. "Witch – witch – I heard something a couple of days ago. I wonder if it means anything."

They looked at her.

She was thinking hard.

"Rumpelstiltskin! That was what I was trying to remember. I was out in my snowshoes, gathering some winter foliage, and I went by that old cabin that's over the hill on the far side of the property." She looked at them to see if they knew what she was talking about. They did.

"That old cabin was once occupied by three women who actually thought they were witches. They were involved in the murder of Percolator Rasmussen back in 2012," Marge told her.

The witches in the cabin had been suspects. Shortly after the murder they had disappeared.

Julie nodded and went on. "When I was walking by the cabin, I heard singing."

"Singing?" Marge asked.

"I slipped up and peeked in the window. There was a little man; he looked just like the picture I had in my head of Rumpelstiltskin, right down to his pointed-toed green shoes. It was by how he danced. He was singing and hopping around a pile of clothes that was like a witch's costume. His song wasn't from the *Rumpelstiltskin* story, though. It was like that one from *The Wizard of Oz*, only different."

They looked confused. Julie looked at them and took a breath and began to sing.

"Ding, dong, the witch is dead. Which old witch? The wicked witch. Ding, dong, the wicked witch is dead."

Julie didn't have a bad voice. She was good. The words weren't exact, but the passion was there.

Marge looked at her, turned, hurried away and in just a few minutes appeared at the back door. "Ron!" She yelled, "Come in here! Haul ass!" The cop turned and started down the path.

He was hauling ass.

"Winifred Wyttch," Hadley said, "Who is she?"

"I don't know," Chaos said softly. "But I killed her. Darn!"

Who Killed Winifred Wyttch?

Ron came through the doors of the dining room and got to the window with long, easy strides. "Ladies," he smiled. Marge introduced them.

Chaos stood up, held her arms out in front of her, wrists together. "I did it," she said. "Cuff me."

Ron smiled. "You've been watching too many television cop shows," he thought for a second and came up with her name..."Ms. Cauldron." The smile went all the way to his eyes.

"No, really," Chaos said. "I asked the powers that be to reign and assault all witches. And there she is. Dead. Darn."

Mary Rose leaned toward Robbie. "Is she raining salt again?"

Robbie shook her head. "She's confessing to murder."

"Oh."

Ron was still smiling. Chaos was still holding her arms out. "Unless you shot her three times in the chest, you probably didn't do her any harm," he said.

"Darn!" Chaos said again and she sat down hard in one of the dining room chairs.

"Three times in the chest?" Marge asked. "That's how cops aim. Point the gun at the main body mass then, if you miss a fatal shot, you're likely to get a serious wound."

Ron nodded.

"Julie!" Marge pointed at the decorator. "Tell him what you saw – Rumpelstiltskin."

Julie told how she had seen the little man in green elf shoes dancing and singing around the pile of witch's clothes.

Ron nodded again.

"I had headquarters run Winifred through the system. Seems she was married to a former cop.

He pulled out his phone and tapped his 'notes' app. "Winifred Wyttch. Married to Glenn Shoue."

Robbie moved toward Marge and Ron. "Wait a minute," she said, "Glenn Shoe?"

"Right," Ron said, "pronounced like the footwear, shoe, but spelled S-h-o-u-e."

Robbie shook her head. "Don't tell me." She put her hand to her head like Johnny Carson used to do when he wore the turban and became Carmac the Magnificent. "Glenn Shoe. His name is…let me think…" she paused for dramatic effect. "His nickname is… 'Gum' Gum Shoe."

"Right again," Ron said. "How'd you know?"

Robbie walked to the window, looked out, raised her arms skyward and said, "Why me, Lord?"

Marge looked at Ron. "She has a thing about weird names."

He nodded again.

So an all-points bulletin went out for Glenn Shoue.

Marge called Ron the Cop every day to see how things were going. True crime made her knee hurt much less. She was absolutely buoyant.

Chaos was both relieved and disappointed that she was not a suspect.

Robbie continued to shake her head and mumble, "Winifred Wyttch and Gum Shoue."

Hadley, on the other hand, took the turkey casserole cook-off seriously. It was to be held the first Sunday in December and she had a secret prize-winning recipe she was entering. In fact, she planned on making two and putting one in the freezer for a dinner party after Christmas.

"I tell you, girls," she said one evening at dinner at Table 12. "That turkey is swooping down and flying off with the prize."

Chaos, who had recovered from her road trip into homicidal guilt, just smiled a small, secret smile.

Spell #2: Roll Casser, Roll!

It had taken Hadley at least three years of making her casserole to pare it down to using less than ten pans, bowls and other kitchen equipment. It was delicious and it always used up all the leftover turkey and dressing and her mouth watered as she started to put it together. Eating a lot of the dressing that went into it was part of the fun.

She hummed Christmas songs as she cut up the turkey into bite-sized pieces. "Hurry up Jingle horse, eight to the beat. Jingle around the clock." While she mixed and nibbled on the dressing, it was, "Nine ladies dancing, eight maids a- milking, seven swans a-swimming, six geese a-laying" and a very loud, "five golden rings!"

She put the casserole into two glass oven dishes, delivered them to a pre-heated oven, washed her hands, filled her dishwasher with her tools of the trade and sat down in her big wing back chair to read. She had just gotten through a James Hankins chapter when she heard the crash.

Crash! Smash! Shatter!

Hadley rushed to the kitchen. One of the glass pans had rolled across the kitchen and smashed up against the wall opposite the oven. She put her hands to her cheeks. Her mouth was open. Turkey casserole was spread in a thick trail all across the kitchen. Steam rose quietly from the sad remains. The glass lay in big pieces all along the turkey trail.

As Hadley watched, the second glass pan teetered on the edge of the oven shelf, then slid quietly to the floor, landing whole and upright. Hadley came out of her stupor, grabbed a tea towel and hurried toward it, slipping in some of the spilled ingredients.

She took hold of the dish, pushed it back into the oven and slammed the door closed. "Stay!" She yelled at it.

She turned, looked at the mess all across the floor and yelled a serious threat.

"Chaos Cauldron! I'm coming for you!"

And she dashed out of her door toward the dining room. Behind her, steam continued to rise from the spilled trail of the prize-winning casserole.

You Turkey!

"That is the most god-awful thing I've ever seen." Alphonso Greatwood was on his scooter, pulled up to Table 12. Sitting around the table were the four girls, Wiley Vondra and Chaos Cauldron. In the center of the table was a turkey or what was supposed to be a turkey.

"Darn!" Chaos said, her arms folded over her chest, her black sweatshirt hiding the one-eyed snake tattoo.

The "turkey" was a 9 x 13 inch glass baking dish. It was sporting a taped-on turkey tail of red, yellow, orange and brown construction paper. Its wings were brown paper and the long neck and head were orange. Yellow construction paper feet were splayed out underneath the dish. It had no eyes and that was probably a good thing. From Alphonso's angle, it was difficult to tell if the head and neck belonged to a turkey or a giraffe.

On the bottom of the dish, in brown magic marker, was written, "Fly, Turkey, Fly! On to Victory!"

"That's the Philadelphia Eagles fight song," Alphonso said, and his big voice bellowed out, "Fly, Eagles, Fly! On the road to Vic-tor-ee!"

They looked at him. Wiley put his head in his hands.

"So all I did was make the turkey and say a spell that it would fly to victory," Chaos whined. She looked miserable.

"The colors are all very autumn-like," Mary Rose said, trying to be kind.

Robbie shook her head; Marge was the one to roll her eyes; and Hadley just stood there, her arms folded in a mirror image of Chaos' and looked at Chaos and the turkey plate.

"We all know these spells don't work," Robbie finally said. "There was some gravitational thing that pulled the casserole out of the oven, some quirk of nature."

"Darn," Chaos said again.

"Chaos, don't try anything else, okay?" Hadley said. Chaos had such an aura of innocence it was hard to stay angry with her.

Chaos nodded and looked contrite.

"No more spells!" Robbie said. Wiley and Alphonso were grinning and watching.

Wiley looked at his friend. "That was the worst rendition of the Eagles fight song I've ever heard. Fly, Eagles, Fly?"

Alphonso grinned. "I always say, 'smile while you still have teeth.'"

"What the hell does that have to do with Fly, Eagles, Fly?"

"I don't know. I just thought of it. After all, you know what an illegal thing is, don't you?"

Wiley stood to follow Alphonso to his office. He shook his head.

"Sick bird."

As the girls started back to their apartments, they walked through the lobby. Without thinking, Hadley walked over and changed the ugly pillows back to where they belonged.

Mary Rose looked out the lobby window. "Look at that wind! I wish I were by a warm lake or even the ocean."

Chaos smiled.

Will they never learn?

Oh Rats!

It was nearly impossible to stay angry at Chaos. She always wore long sleeves, so the snake tattoo wasn't bothering Robbie. Her "Darn!" was charming in a strange, innocent way and she simply was who she was – no pretense, no faking.

Once or twice a week, they all met in Hadley's apartment for popcorn with goldfish crackers and M&Ms and champagne. A new and very large supply of both had been set in, hoping against hope there would not be more snow for a while.

On those afternoons, Chaos started bringing Double-Double, Toil and Trouble. As in real life, the rats were winning the race.

"They really are kind of cute," Mary Rose said the first time Chaos brought them. She also brought three little thimbles and poured some champagne for each of them.

They drank it.

They felt good.

Rat-like inhibitions disappeared.

Geoffrey didn't get any champagne. The first time the rats appeared, dressed in their tiny red, white and blue sweaters, he watched them.

He drooled.

He sniffed the air.

Then, when Toil jumped off Chaos' lap and onto the floor, he pounced. His mouth went around the rat's head and his tail began to wag. He lay down, ready for a tasty rat snack.

Then the yelling began.

"Geoff! No!"

"Geoffrey, put him down! Spit him out!"

"Darn! Darn!"

"Bad dog! Bad, bad dog!"

All his ladies, except Marge, were on their feet, yelling and waving their arms. Marge was pounding the floor with her cane.

Bad dog. He was being bad dog.

Geoffrey's mouth opened. Toil backed out, tripping over the big mastiff's tongue on his way to safety.

The other two rats were on the floor, ready to rescue their brother. They were sitting up, eyes a little blurred from the champagne, but teeth bared and fur raised. Little paws were held in front of them, like little boxers.

Geoffrey looked from one of his women to the next. It was bad dog to eat these rats. He looked pitiful. The rats looked ready to kill him. His people looked mad.

Bad dog, bad, bad dog.

He lay down, his head between his paws. He would be hit now. He had been beaten when he was with the mean man, Thorny Busch, but Mary Rose had never hit him.

He prepared for a bad, bad beating.

Then Mary Rose did something strange. She picked up Toil and brought him over by Geoffrey. With a lot of effort and creaking somewhere in her bones, she sat down on the floor beside her dog and stroked his big head.

"It's okay, Geoff. You just did your doggie thing."

Mary Rose didn't hit him. Instead, she cupped her hands. Toil's head popped out between her fingers.

He looked at Geoffrey with a scowl. Then he mellowed and stretched his little head out. Geoffrey looked at the stupid rat and then at his lady. He knew what to do. He leaned over and sniffed the tasty rat. Guess what. It smelled like–rat.

He looked up at his ladies. They were smiling because a dog had licked a rat.

Human intelligence is highly overrated.

"Good dog, Geoffrey!"

"Good, good doggie."

"Isn't that sweet?"

"Darn, that's nice."

Geoffrey licked the stupid rat's head, farted and lay down his own head again. He would never understand people. And what is this dressing up animals anyway? Rats in sweaters? He drooled again, burped and closed his eyes.

Swat isn't Just for Flies

There was no sign or word of Glenn "Gum" Shoe. One day, when the remaining snow was only on the lawns or in big mountains in the shopping center parking lots, the girls decided to put on their boots and go take a look at the cabin where Julie had seen the probably–Glenn person singing.

The sun was under a cloud. It was not horribly cold and their heavy jackets, gloves and boots kept them warm. Mary Rose and Marge both wore hats. Chaos had on her bright purple stocking cap and purple jacket. Robbie and Hadley were bare-headed and thinking how hats would have been a good idea. Geoffrey, on the other hand, was bouncing along beside them, jumping from snow bank to snow bank along the sidewalk. It was good outdoors for good dogs.

The cabin was about a quarter mile from Meadow Lakes. Marge had taken three aspirin to keep her knee from holding her back and, as they walked along, they laughed and warmed up, walking as briskly as they could.

The little sidewalk twisted around from the back of Meadow Lakes, past a block of diminutive houses and ended in a small woods. The cabin sat back, deep in the little woods, several yards from where the sidewalk stopped.

The trees were bare now, the snow still deep, the bushes still covered with their white decoration from nature. The girls waded through the snow with the big mastiff bouncing along beside them.

"This snow is getting into the tops of my boots, for Pete's sake," Robbie complained.

"Next time, buy those sexy thigh-high boots, girl," Hadley joked. The snow was slipping into the tops of her boots, too. Marge nodded. Only Chaos had the high- top winter boots that worked in this weather.

They stopped when they came to the cabin. The paint had disappeared years ago. The shutters were hanging in dismay. The front porch had holes in the floor and the front steps were obviously unsafe and ready to fall in. The roof looked particularly fragile.

"It has all the charm of a boarded-up Kmart," Hadley said.

Robbie nodded.

"Listen," Marge whispered.

They listened.

From inside the house they could hear a country western radio station with a cowboy singing how his girlfriend was going to take her love to town.

"Obviously a smart woman," Robbie whispered to Hadley.

"Be careful," Marge whispered, and she began to walk into the woods, keeping several trees between the girls and the cabin. Her cell phone was in her hand.

They walked, making a little path with their tracks, to a spot not far from the cabin.

A huge, untrimmed hedge hid them from the dark and dirty windows looking out into the trees. Inside, they could make out the shadow of someone moving around.

Geoffrey whined.

"I'm going closer," Marge said. "You stay here."

The girls stopped in their tracks.

Geoffrey sat.

All except Geoffrey were happy to stay where they were.

"Watch out, Marge," Hadley whispered as their friend went farther around through the trees so she could approach the cabin from behind, unseen.

In just a few minutes she appeared again, sliding along the side of the house, her red cane ready for anything, including helping her keep her balance.

She slipped silently up to the window and peeked in. She looked for a second, then began to slide back along the wall toward the back of the cabin. In just minutes, she was back beside the girls, breathing a little heavily.

"It's him," she said. Geoffrey wagged his tail in agreement.

She took out her cell phone and called Ron the Cop.

"We'll stay here," Marge said, "and make sure he doesn't leave."

They were pretty sure Ron the Cop had told her to get back to Meadow Lakes pronto, but they stayed, moving their eyes from the window to the front porch, back to the window, then to the back porch. Geoffrey dug furiously in the snow, finding nothing.

Gummy was staying inside and not leaving. Now the singing cowboy was moaning about his horse that died and his girl who ran off. Probably on another horse.

"I'm getting cold," Mary Rose whispered.

"Me, too," Robbie whispered back.

They couldn't be seen behind the big bushes that were cooperative enough to have openings through which they could peer at the cabin.

Chaos and Marge didn't move. They looked as if they were enjoying a spring day at Memorial Park.

BOOB Girls, super spies – with guard dog.

Just when Robbie and Hadley were ready to suggest they move their frozen feet toward home, a large black van with SWAT on the side pulled up in front of the cabin. They could see the probably-Gummy jump out of his chair and look out the front window, just as the first boots hit the porch steps. A big officer smashed through the door, shoulder first. The door crashed to the floor. Four SWAT members followed, guns aimed and ready.

Ron the Cop was walking slowly toward the porch.

Marge ducked further down behind the bushes.

They saw a flash and heard a boom from inside. The cabin, which was ancient and not all that well built to begin with, sagged and part of the roof slid off onto the ground close to where the girls were hiding. The windows blew out and ugly-looking smoke drifted toward them. Another crash inside sounded as if a floor had collapsed. They ducked to hide even further. Geoffrey snuggled up to Mary Rose.

Several minutes passed.

"I can't stay bent over like this much longer," Mary Rose whispered.

There was yelling from inside. They could hear "Clear!" Then "Clear!" Then "Clear" again. Suddenly, everything was quiet.

Ron the Cop came out the front door, looked at the roof lying on the ground, then at the front door. The SWAT team came out, one at a time.

There was no Gum Shoue with them.

Two of the team moved cautiously to the back of the cabin, one on each side of the wrecked building.

Nothing.

The team gathered around Ron the Cop who was shaking his head. "We'll check the woods," they heard him say.

Marge raised her cane into the air so Ron the Cop could see it. He squinted, shook his head and smiled.

"Let's wait a few minutes," he said. It looked as if he was speaking to the overgrown hedgerow where they were hiding.

"Follow me," Marge whispered. She turned and, still bent low, slipped slowly into the woods. Mary Rose had hold of Geoffrey's collar. She straightened up and the girls did the same as Marge began to walk as fast as she could through the snow.

"It's probably not a good time to remind us to S.H.I.T. is it?" Mary Rose asked.

Both Hadley and Robbie shook their heads and straightened up as best they could.

They heard Chaos whisper, "Darn!" as she tripped over a fallen branch.

"I just didn't think old age would come so fast," Hadley said, putting her hand to the middle of her back.

They found the sidewalk and took the long way back to Meadow Lakes, easily avoiding the SWAT team.

"He wasn't there," Marge said, when they settled into Hadley's apartment, boots off, feet warming on footstools and bodies warming with hot chocolate.

"He didn't come out," Hadley said. "At least, we didn't see him."

"And we had a full view of everything," Robbie added.

"So, where did he go?" Mary Rose asked.

"Beats me," Marge replied, her cane lying across her lap like a tired puppy.

"Darn!" Chaos said. That pretty well said it all.

Three days passed and there was no sign of Glenn 'Gum' Shoue. Ron the Cop had called Marge and scolded her soundly for being at the cabin. It was working pretty well until he started laughing and hung up.

It was another snowy afternoon, just before Christmas. They were at Table 12, half way through a game of Big Bang Theory Monopoly (Mary Rose with Amy's tiara was winning as usual). Because it wasn't meal time, Geoffrey was allowed in the dining room and was sleeping under the table and dreaming of treeing cats and annoying rats. Alphonso and Wiley had disappeared into Alphonso's office and the girls were alone in the big dining room.

The big door from the kitchen pantry area opened

and a man in a white kitchen coat came through and headed toward the kitchen.

"Look," Chaos said, "even the cooks are dressing for the holidays. See those neat little green elf shoes that cook is wearing?"

Marge froze, the dice in her hand suspended in mid-air.

"Green elf shoes?" She whispered. "Look, but don't let him see you."

Marge and Chaos looked at the cook; Mary Rose slid sideways in her chair and pretended to pick something up off the floor; Robbie stood up and stretched and looked and Hadley turned the wrong way and got a view out the window. Geoffrey opened one eye and farted.

"Where?" Hadley whispered.

"It's Shoue," Marge said, so softly they could barely hear her. "He's going into the kitchen."

As soon as the kitchen door swung shut, Marge's cell phone was out and she was speed-dialing Ron the Cop. The other girls looked at her. She pointed toward the kitchen, then at the two doors opening into it at each end.

They got the drift. Divide and make a major effort to conquer. Geoffrey got the drift, too. "Play!" He stayed close to Mary Rose, doggie tense and ready for action.

"Ron the Cop won't like this," Hadley said to Robbie as they headed toward the door through which Gummy had disappeared.

Robbie nodded.

Mary Rose, Geoffrey and Marge were headed toward the door at the far end of the kitchen with Chaos staying a safe distance behind.

"What if he's armed?" Mary Rose whispered.

"So are we," Marge said, brandishing her red cane.

Geoffrey growled his best growl.

Good dog, Geoffrey!

They opened the swinging doors at the same time and burst in, at least as fast as ladies their age can burst. Gummy was at the refrigerator, taking out the last ingredients for a ham and cheese sandwich.

He looked up, total surprise on his face.

Hadley grabbed a skillet from the drying table.

Robbie grabbed a long-handled soup pan from beside it.

Mary Rose picked up a huge cast-iron frying pan and Marge pointed her cane at Shoue.

"Freeze!" She yelled.

Geoffrey stopped dead in his tracks. He froze, just like his Marge woman said.

Chaos ducked behind a second table and kept repeating, "Darn!" over and over under her breath.

Gum Shoue didn't freeze. He made a run for the exit door, moving very fast toward Marge, obviously intending to knock her down before she could hit him with the cane. She planned to taser him, but he didn't know about the red cane and he didn't care. He was on a dangerous collision course with a large lady.

"Play!", Geoffrey thought, and he took two long mastiff leaps and did a flying jump onto the running man.

Marge shot the taser.

She hit Geoffrey in the butt.

The force of the hit carried the big mastiff onto Gummy's chest and face, knocking Shoue flat on his back on the kitchen floor. Geoffrey's tongue was hanging out and Shoue couldn't move. He was totally still from the waist up; his feet were scrambling for traction. He was trying to lift his arms to push Geoffrey's body off and was making good progress. In just seconds, he was sitting up, the limp body of the big dog pushed down across his legs.

That was when Mary Rose reached him.

"You killed my doggie!" She yelled and she took a batter's stance, held the skillet with both hands and hit Glenn Shoue upside the head with a knockout, home run blow.

Mary Rose McGill, batting 1,000.

He went back down. If he had been a cartoon character, there would have been little x's for his eyes.

The doors opened and Alphonso came rushing in on his scooter, Wiley Vondra right behind him.

"What the hell is going on?" he yelled. "We could hear you clear in my office."

"He killed Winifred Wyttch," Marge explained. She was speaking loudly.

"And he made Marge taser Geoffrey," Mary Rose whined. She was patting Geoffrey, who would also have had x's for eyes. He was breathing, but Mary Rose was still close to tears.

"If Geoffrey were smarter, he could tell us what he needs." She was kneeling on the floor beside the big, still body.

"If you were smarter, he wouldn't have to," Wiley said, just a touch of anger in his voice.

"Wiley Vondra, get your skinny ass over here and help me up!" Mary Rose said.

Wiley got his skinny ass over and helped her up.

"You women have a habit of beating people up in my retirement community," Alphonso said. You couldn't tell whether he was angry or proud.

Hey – who needs security personnel when you have four tough widows?

Chaos had slipped out from her hiding place and was acting as if she'd been part of it all. "Mary Rose gave him a knockout blow, all right," she said.

Ron the Cop and three uniforms had responded to Marge's call. They hurried through the door and took in the scene. Ron looked, grinned and said, "Excuse me."

He turned and walked back through the door and they could hear him laugh. In less than two minutes, he came back into the kitchen, serious and business like.

The uniformed officers handcuffed Glenn Shoue and pulled him to his feet. Ron hugged Marge, gave a thumbs-up sign to Alphonso and Wiley, nodded to the girls and left behind the uniforms and a woozy Shoue.

They stood alone in the kitchen.

"Grandmothers don't do this!" Wiley Vondra said.

"Partly correct," Hadley said. "Some grandmothers bake cookies."

"Some grandmothers do crafts," Robbie said.

"Some grandmothers take care of their grandchildren," Marge added.

They looked at Chaos. She shrugged. "They watch soap operas?"

"But some grandmothers take down bad guys and beat the crap out of them," Mary Rose said, slamming down the skillet onto the nearest table. The sound echoed through the spotless kitchen.

Alphonso grinned. "I know what you say, 'Never underestimate a burned out old broad.' You want a little glass of wine in my office, ladies?"

"We'll have wine," Hadley said. "But remember, size does matter. No one wants a little glass of wine."

We Wish You A . . . . .

Hadley had won the leftover turkey casserole contest. All the girls had entered a recipe. And you're right – they're all in the back of this book under Cluck and Gobble.

Her prize had been a tiny brass turkey which lived now on her end table.

Christmas came. Each BOOB Girl had different thoughts and memories.

Hadley remembered how her surrogate grandson, Nick, had climbed on a high ladder to put lights on the peak over the doorway of her big house in the suburbs.

Marge remembered making sugar cookies with her daughter. She had cut out a cookie bell and laid it to one side. Her little three-year-old had looked, picked the cookie up, said, "Puzzle!" and put it back into the rolled-out dough.

Mary Rose remembered cooking a huge dinner for four daughters, their husbands and three grandchildren, plus her quiet, not-at-all-helpful husband. She was relieved that she would never have to do that again.

Robbie remembered decorating her Old Market apartment and how her husband had tied a Christmas bell on his wheelchair, held mistletoe over his head and given her a sweet, tender kiss.

Wiley remembered Christmas in Korea and all its bleakness.

Alphonso remembered playing a Christmas Day football game years ago with the Kansas City Chiefs when the wind chill on the field was fifteen degrees below zero. He put on his warmest Chief's sweater.

Hadley's son and his current wife appeared, along with one granddaughter who spent most of the time texting friends.

Marge's children were on duty in Chicago, but both called her.

Mary Rose's four Marys appeared with their families and Mary Rose was glad again she didn't have to cook.

Robbie, Wiley and Alphonso were without family, so they made one with the girls and their children.

"You don't always find your family under the roof where you were born,"

Robbie quoted. Then she said, "Richard Bach in Jonathan Livingston Seagull – I think."

It had been a good day. Meadow Lakes was so decked out in Christmas that none of the girls had bothered with a tree this year. Each had a fun wreath on her door and exchanged small gifts.

Robbie unwrapped a beautiful Navajo ring with four different stones from Raven. She slipped it on her right hand. It fit perfectly. She knew it would never come off.

As the evening slipped in and the moon slipped out from behind a cloud, there was a knock on Robbie's door.

"Come in," she called; sure it was one of the girls. A long shadow crossed her living room and stood in the door of her bedroom where she sat in bed, reading a book on her tablet.

She smiled.

"Hey, Raven," she said.

Raven, the handsome Apache, took off his jacket and threw it on the chair beside the bed. Then he began to unbutton his shirt.

Robbie put the tablet down and took off her glasses and held up her hand wearing the ring.

Spell #3 – You Look Flushed

Bored: feeling weary because you are unoccupied
Bored: not knowing what you want to do
Bored: being totally uninteresting or interested

Mary Rose McGill was bored. It was snowing again. After all, it was Nebraska. The sky was a dull, wintry gray, promising still more snow. Even the wind had hidden behind the big fir trees and refused to come out.

She had tried to get interested in the latest Stephen King novel, but even good old Stephen lacked his usual mayhem and suspense today. Mary Rose wondered if he ever got bored. She wondered if she should go to Robbie's apartment and ask to watch The Walking Dead. That's what it feels like when you're bored.

She sighed, put down her tablet where Stephen lived while she read him and went to the bathroom. "Most exciting thing I've done today," she thought.

She finished and flushed the toilet.

Meadow Lakes was a somewhat upscale retirement community. This was an upscale toilet. The water rose gently into the bowl – and then it kept rising. Mary Rose watched as it came to the rim and quietly rushed over onto the floor, immediately soaking the red and yellow rugs by the sink and tub.

It kept coming.

"What?!" Mary Rose yelled at it. "Are you related to the Sorcerer's Apprentice or something?"

She flushed it again.

The toilet didn't answer. It just kept spewing water onto the floor with gentle determination. Mary Rose backed out of the bathroom, her shoes leaving wet little footprints in her beige carpet. She hurried to her chair where her cell phone lay.

"Wiley Vondra, get your ass over here!" Mary Rose said into the phone, louder than usual. "My bathroom is flooded!"

In the meantime, Geoffrey, who was never bored, sensed something interesting and trotted into the bathroom. The water completely covered his big paws. He looked around and started lapping up the flood. In just a minute, dampness dripping from his chin, he raised his head, glanced at the toilet and back at the water. Then he lay down and rolled from side to side, back and forth on the soaked floor.

It felt great!

Mary Rose threw her phone onto the chair and hurried into the laundry room to grab her cheap sponge mop; then she hurried back to the bathroom. Geoffrey jumped up and delivered a massive shake just as she got into range. The spray of water went onto the wall and as far into the room as the top of the bed. It soaked the front of Mary Rose's jeans and shirt.

"Crap!"

Shake, shake, grin, grin. "Woof!"

Mary Rose started to mop as fast as she could.

Mop; squeeze the water out into the sink, Mop. Squeeze.

"This is like eating a pot roast with a toothpick!"

Geoffrey lapped some more and shook again.

This was fun.

Wonder dog at work.

"Crap!" again, as the mop caught in the emergency pull chain that was in every bedroom and bathroom in the senior living complex. A call would go directly to 911, but Mary Rose switched it off immediately.

"Crap!"

"Having a fun time?" Wiley stood in the bathroom doorway, arms folded, leaning against the door jab. He had a stupid-looking grin that looked suspiciously like the one Geoffrey was wearing, on his face.

"Have you got a plunger?" Mary Rose asked.

"Isn't this why we have guys called 'maintenance,' so we don't need things like plungers?"

"I want to do it myself!"

Wiley headed toward the door to get a plunger. Mary Rose could hear him talking to someone. She kept on mopping.

In just a few minutes he was back.

"I don't have a plunger. I called maintenance. By the way, the fire department was here."

Mary Rose stopped mopping and walked to the bedroom window. A fire truck with flashing lights was just pulling away from the entrance.

"You've got to be kidding!"

"Nope, opened the door and a fireman was there. Asked if we had called 911."

"And you didn't call me? Was he cute?"

"There were three of them."

"Three of them! Were they cute?"

"Yeah. They were young. They were in shape. They have muscles. They climb up tall ladders carrying big hoses."

"And you didn't call me?" Mary Rose was almost yelling.

She stopped when Alphonso rode through the door on his scooter, plunger held high above his head like an Olympic torch. A sign in magic marker on a sheet of typing paper was taped to the front of the Green Machine and read "Maintenance Rescue."

Without even looking at Wiley and Mary Rose, he drove into the bathroom, made one plunge into the bowl, turned and drove back out, plunger torch held high and Geoffrey bouncing along beside him. He zoomed by Wiley and Mary Rose, grinning like an idiot and still not saying a word. His scooter wheels made a wet track all the way to the door. Beside the tracks were giant paw prints.

Super hero saves the day!

"You flushed the toilet when it was overflowing to see if it would go down, didn't you?" Wiley put his arm around Mary Rose's shoulders.

"Sometimes that works."

"No it doesn't," Wiley said. "You know, last week someone asked me what one word I would use to describe you." He smiled into her squinted eyes. "Honest to God, 'Nutcase' did not come to my mind."

He walked quickly out the door, careful not to step in the wet paw prints, and caught up with Alphonso.

Wisely, neither of them laughed out loud.

Chaos was quiet and contrite when Mary Rose told them about the flood. Finally, Mary Rose stopped talking and looked at her.

"Chaos?" she said.

"I did it again, darn it!" Chaos said. "Remember when you said you wished you were at the beach?"

Mary Rose looked confused. "That was a long time ago, I don't really remember."

"Well, I made a happy water spell. My spells are kind of slow moving."

They looked at her.

In the meantime, the chairs in the lobby sported the wrong pillows again.

"Okay," Robbie smiled. "We don't believe your spells, Chaos. If you can do a spell, give me a man – preferably Raven – and a bank. I want to take a trip with that Indian and I need funds."

Raven had stayed three days and he and Robbie had left her apartment only for meals and a quick trip to the Old Market. It had been a wonderful, delightful, rewarding time and Robbie felt loved and renewed. Raven felt tired and good. She had no idea when he would appear again.

"Apache Indian tricks," he had told her.

Spell #4: Three Men and A Bank

Winter had loosened its grip on Omaha and the Northern Plains. Things were back to normal and normal was good. The sun was high in the sky when the girls decided to go to lunch at their favorite place.

"I'm going to scoot behind the wheel and make a quick trip to the bank over on Dodge," Robbie said, as Marge pulled the Hummer up in front of Marks Bistro. "I need to get some cash for lunch and to buy some stuff afterwards."

"Works for me," Marge said from behind the wheel.

The three girls got out. Robbie walked around the Hummer and got behind the wheel. Hadley blew a kiss to the Hummer as it moved down Underwood Street to take Robbie eleven blocks to their local bank.

It was such a pleasant day now that most of the snow had been removed and the streets were clear again. It was good to get out. Robbie turned up the radio and let the classical music of KVNO fill the big vehicle. Otis XII, her favorite DJ wasn't at the station at this hour, but his deep, recorded voice was letting her know that she definitely had the Omaha area's classical station.

There was a short line of cars at the drive through window. Robbie didn't want to wait. She would get out and go inside where her favorite young tellers would have cheery words and smiles for her.

As she opened her driver's side door, she heard the unmistakable sound of the passenger door opening as well. She turned and looked. A tall, heavyset, homely man in his mid-forties was climbing into the Hummer. And there was no mistake about it. There was a gun in his gloved hand. His one boot that was already on the floor mat was covered with slush and snow. He was surrounded by a foul, unwashed smell. Robbie held her breath for a few seconds, then, following the motion he made with the gun, slid back into the driver's seat.

He looked at her.

"That your ATM?" he asked, twisting his ugly head toward the big ATM machine that stood as part of the bank's drive-through.

A hundred thoughts went through Robbie's head and she felt her heart go out of rhythm and start to beat faster and raggedly. With only a second to decide what to do, she looked directly at him. His eyes were squinted, his face wrinkled and his head shaved. She could see part of a tattoo on his neck. She gathered her courage and began to turn into an actress.

"It is my ATM," she said with more confidence than she felt. She looked serious and afraid.

That part was easy. She felt serious and afraid.

"But I don't have any money there." (Tears in her eyes) "I just went through a terrible time. My husband died. (Loud sniff – head held down)

Robinson Leary, academy award nominee.

"You got any money in that bank?"

(Head still down) "No," her voice dropped to a whisper. "I was going in to see if I could get a loan so I wouldn't have to sell my car."

"My God, Lady! You drive a Hummer!"

"Oh," (looking up with a pitiful expression) "it belongs to a friend. My car is a 2004 Dodge with well over one hundred thousand miles on it." (Pause, sniff) "And it needs new tires!" She wailed the last sentence and dropped her head on the steering wheel. "My friend who owns this Hummer is a retired homicide detective. She makes good money and has offered to help me, but you know how you hate to ask for help. It's just awful."

The man nodded.

"There are other things I can do," he said, looking her up and down and making an obscene motion with his hips.

"Oh, you can," Robbie said. "But if you rape me, I'll have to have years and years of therapy and I don't have money for therapy and I don't know if I'll even do okay in it. Some therapists just don't know anything."

"Tell me about it," the man nodded again.

"But I can take you to a place where I know there is money and even drugs." She whispered the last two words as she leaned toward him, holding her breath so her nose wouldn't be offended.

She gave him her most earnest, sincere look. He made another motion with his gun that told her to drive off.

She drove off.

She eased out of her parking space and headed toward the bank's parking lot entrance. At the entrance she looked both ways, and with a smooth motion, reached into her pocket and found her cell phone. As she did, from the corner of her eye she noticed the open peanut package Marge had slipped into the map holder on the side of the door.

She leaned out to check oncoming traffic and at the same time she hit Marge's speed dial number. She had pressed it so often she was pretty sure she pressed it right this time, too.

Just as Marge answered, Robbie began to talk loudly and Otis XII on the radio joined in with a pre-recorded commercial.

"So even though you tried to rob me to get me to get money from the bank and were probably going to rape me, I'm happy to take you to 515 South 15th Street where you can have all the money and drugs and anything else you need.

The man was silent.

Fifteenth Street was right in front of them. When Robbie lived in the Old Market, she had walked by number 515 many times.

Robbie turned right. A large grey building came into view.

"Jesus, Lady! That's the friggin' police station!"

Robbie grabbed the open peanut pack and threw it at his eyes.

Direct hit!

"Hey! Dammit, there's salt in there!" He rubbed his eyes, opened them and looked at her with a surprised expression.

He tried the door.

Locked.

He pushed the button to lower the window. The window lowered quickly with a smooth motion.

Automobile technology at its best.

Robbie speeded up even more.

He tried to climb out the window, his butt looking too big to get through the small space, even as big as it was on the Hummer.

Robbie reached out and grabbed his pants pocket. He struggled. His pants were low on his butt and slipped down around his knees.

He tried getting through the window again.

He pushed on the seat with his feet.

Robbie zigged and zagged the Hummer, keeping him off balance.

He made it.

Just as Robbie slammed on the brakes at the back door of the police station and jail, he toppled out, butt naked, directly into the arms of two uniforms who were waiting for him.

Robbie spoke toward her pocket where Marge was still on the phone.

"I have to go in and file a report, Marge. You girls go ahead and eat. Bring me some mac and cheese to go, will you, and I'll pick you up as soon as I'm done here."

She climbed out, shaking her head. She sighed. "Things are just going to the dogs around here."

Robinson Leary, girl philosopher.

She followed the two policemen and the smelly man with the large, bare rear into the big station at 515 South 15th Street where, inside, there certainly were both drugs and money, just as she had promised.

Robbie picked up her friends at Marks. They had ordered her the big mac and cheese, Mark's specialty. She told them what had happened.

They looked at Chaos.

She shrugged.

Doctor My Eyes Have Seen all the Years (1972 song by Jackson Browne)

There is a delightful retired weatherman from San Diego who talks about how men age. He says something like, "You see an old man and you can tell at some time his face has said, 'I'm tired of being a face. I think I'll be a neck,' and it slips down and becomes a wattle. Then his manly chest says, 'That's a good idea. I think I'll move south and become a stomach.'"

We change. We have ills and pills and medical bills. As one friend said, "At my age, I make a lot of new friends. Most of them have 'MD' behind their names."

And so it was that our four heroines decided they would all go together when one of them had a doctor's appointment. Chaos, being one of the smarter ones, passed, saying simply, "No thanks. Darned if I'll do doctors!"

"She doesn't 'do doctors,'" Mary Rose said.

"She's healthy," Marge said.

"She's lucky," Robbie said.

Hadley did an eyeroll.

The BOOB Girls. Wellness philosophers.

First up was Hadley, who was scheduled for an eye appointment with her retinal specialist, Dr. Ed McGillacudy. This often meant she would get a shot in the eye.

That's right – not FOR the eye, IN the eye

They arrived at Dr. McGillacudy's office right on time.

Hellos and several hugs were waiting for Hadley. She joked with Janice at the front desk, hugged Tarah when she walked into the waiting room and, in just minutes, Stephanie called her in and gave her yet another hug.

The girls followed her in and took seats side by side in a second waiting room. Hadley was called into a tiny room by a handsome young man named Jarred who, of course, gave her a hug.

Hadley Joy Morris-Whitfield, queen of hugs.

"Nice buns," Mary Rose said as Jarred closed the door behind Hadley.

"Mary Rose McGill!" Robbie said, faking a shocked look.

Hadley had pictures of her retinas taken with a big device called an Optical Coherent Tomographer.

"As far as I'm concerned, it's the only coherent thing about macular degeneration, Hadley said when she came out and sat down with her friends.

The waiting room was bordered by private examination rooms. In the waiting area itself, two rows of reasonably comfortable chairs faced each other. A third row made up the far end facing the exam rooms. The four friends moved their chairs around so they could see over Robbie's shoulder as she sat with her iPad on her lap. Across and to the side, patients who were also waiting were looking at magazines, playing with their phones, reading from tablets or, in more than one case – dozing.

"Okay, girls, here's the plan. I have a fun email. I'm going to read the questions and," she looked around and saw Mary Rose close by her left arm, "and when I point to you, Mary Rose, you read the answer. It's from the old television show, 'Hollywood Squares.'"

"I remember Hollywood Squares," Hadley, Marge and two people across from them said together. The people across the room said it very softly, then turned and gave each other embarrassed smiles.

A woman spoke up, "Who was on that? Wasn't Phyllis Diller one of the Squares?"

"Oh, and Rose Marie, who was on the Dick Van Dyke show," Mary Rose added.

"My favorite was Charlie Weaver," a man spoke up. They were speaking a little louder now.

"One time I saw Groucho Marx on it," Marge said.

Robbie cleared her throat. Now nearly everyone in the waiting room was listening.
"Question: Do female frogs croak?"

She pointed to Mary Rose who leaned in and read Charlie Weaver's answer. "If you hold their little heads under water long enough."

Several people chuckled.

Robbie read the next question, "If you're going to make a parachute jump, how high should you be?"

She pointed to Marge this time, who leaned toward the computer and said, "Three days of steady drinking should do it." It had been Charlie Weaver's answer again.

This time everyone in the waiting room laughed a little. A sleeping man snorted awake and looked around, confused.

Robbie read on, "A pea can last up to 50 years. True or false?"

This time Mary Rose gave the answer given years ago by George Gobel, "Boy, it sure seems that way sometimes."

The entire room was attentive. Hadley, who couldn't see because her eyes were dilated, was laughing the hardest.

Robbie: "You're having trouble going to sleep. Are you probably a man or a woman?"

Marge read Don Knott's answer: "That's what's been keeping me awake." She looked around. "I loved Don Knotts!"

"Best deputy Mayberry, USA ever had," a balding gentleman at the end of the row chirped in.

Robbie: "According to Cosmopolitan Magazine, if you meet a stranger at a party, is it okay to ask if he's married?"

Mary Rose answered for Rose Marie, "No. It's better to wait until morning."

Everyone laughed. One lady applauded.

Mary Rose McGill, Hollywood Squares wannabe.

"Next one is for Rose Marie, too," Robbie said. She looked at Mary Rose. "You're going bowling. What is the perfect score?"

Mary Rose grinned a big grin and looked at the crowd, "Ralph the Pin Boy." The room roared and everyone was awake.

Tarah came for one patient and the lady refused to go into the examining room until she heard the next question.

It was a good one.

"According to Ann Landers, is it alright to kiss people you just met?"

Marge answered for Charlie Weaver, "It kept me out of the army."

The lady went into the examining room laughing. So did Tarah.

"The last question is for Paul Lynde," Robbie said, pointing to Marge.

"According to Ann Landers, what are two things you should never do in bed?"

Marge had the answer. "Point and laugh," she said.

A white-haired man on the corner spoke up. "Remember when the question was, "In a tornado, are you safer under the bed, in the bedroom or in a closet?"

His elderly wife punched his arm and said, "I'm always safe in the bedroom."

Three people applauded. The others laughed.

"Have you got just one more?" a younger woman in the middle of the row across from them asked. She was a twenty-five year old hard body. She worked out.

Robbie smiled. "Jackie Gleason recently revealed he firmly believes in them and has seen them on at least two occasions. What are they?"

Marge answered for George Gobel, "His feet."

Everyone laughed except the young woman who had asked for one more question.

She looked puzzled, "Who's Jackie Gleason?"

Kids today!

"This is really the last one," Robbie said, looking around the room. "Which of your senses diminishes as you grow older?"

Mary Rose answered for Charlie Weaver, "My sense of decency."

There was a pause after the laughter. Everything was quiet for about three minutes. Tarah, Stephanie and Jarred hurried in to get people to examining rooms before they insisted on staying for the next joke. When Tarah called Hadley into the examining room, the other three crowded in with her. Dr. Ed looked a little surprised, then grinned and welcomed them. He was an attractive man, thin, with a suit that looked one size too big. He peered into Hadley's eyes through a big scope and announced that a shot would indeed be in order. "One more shot should bring that under control," he announced.

Hadley had fainted at the first shot, been a little woozy at the second, then took the rest like the trooper she was.

"You ladies want to get around where you can watch?" Ed asked.

Marge moved in close beside the chair so she could see every move and get a good view of Hadley's right eye. Hadley reached out and took hold of Marge's hand.

Robbie and Mary Rose looked at each other. Mary Rose made a quick motion toward the door with her head and the two of them skeedaddled back into the waiting room.

One BOOB Girl who fainted was enough for them.

"Peep, peep, peep," the man with the other tablet said when they hurriedly sat down. "Chickens!"

They nodded and became pale.

When they left the doctor's office, they went immediately to Marks for lunch. They each had a glass of good wine, Hadley wearing her dark, dark glasses all through the meal.

How Can You Mend a Broken Heart? (Bee Gees, 1971)

In just a week, they were in a doctor's office again. This time it was Robbie, who had an annual appointment with her cardiologist. Her heart kept popping in and out of sinus rhythm and she had tried everything from cardioversions – an electric jolt – to different meds.

Didn't seem to matter.

"It's a party heart," she said once. "It only goes out at night."

That wasn't always true. It had popped out when she had delivered the would-be car-jacker to the police station, but had gone back to normal by the time she got to Marks. Now she was wired for an EKG, which Rebecca was doing with flare and some lame jokes.

She looked down at Robbie. "Does an apple a day keep the doctor away?" she asked with a grin as she put another sticky pad on Robbie's chest.

"OK – I'll bite," Robbie said. "No pun intended. Does an apple a day keep the doctor away?"

"Only if you aim it right," Rebecca replied.

Anne, Robbie's nurse and friend, stuck her head in the door. "Aim for the head, then, if your doctor is a zombie, you'll kill it."

They laughed and groaned.

When doctor Easley walked in, they were still smiling. Easley was an attractive, mixed race man who some patients called, "Dr. Hottie." He hugged Robbie, who was sitting up in the big chair now, and she introduced him to her friends.

Coming in the door directly behind him was a young Indian man in a white coat.

"This is Deepa," Dr. Easley said. "He's observing today and spending a few months here at the Med Center."

The young man nodded at them and smiled. They smiled back.

He stood with his hands behind his back and didn't move or say a word.

Obviously, very good at observing.

"Things look good, my dear," Easley said. "Keep on keeping on." He offered Robbie his hand to help her up and gave her a hug. The other girls lined up for hugs as well. He obliged and they all laughed.

Then Robbie looked at young Deepa. "You are a long way from home," she said, "and if your grandmother is still alive and in India, she misses you. Today, I'll be your grandmother. Come get a Grandma hug."

The young doctor broke into a delightful grin. "My grandmother IS still in India and I miss her very much."

In three big steps he was in Robbie's hug. He stepped back from her, said, "Thank you," turned and walked straight into the door.

Easley looked surprised, then smiled.

"I'm all right," Deepa said. "I'm all right."

He and Dr. Easley left. Easley turned and winked at the girls.

Marge turned to Robbie. "Whatever it is," she said, "you still have it, girl."

Silicone Grown (Rod Stewart and the Faces, 1973)

It was good to get all the doctor time done in one month. Next up was Mary Rose McGill, scheduled for a mammogram and exam by her oncologist. In 2010, Mary Rose had breast cancer.

Yep, **Boob Girls Book II: Lies, Spies and Cinnamon Rolls.**

She had gotten on her computer and asked for tasteless jokes, tacky cards and lots of prayers and support. She had gotten them. When she took chemotherapy treatments, Calamity Doodles, the newest BOOB Girl, had taken a page from her father's clown playbook, dressed them all up and performed a showstopping clown act in the chemo room, with all the nurses and techs wearing red noses.

When Calamity got stuck while doing the splits, with both legs frozen to the floor, she had been carried out waving and to wild applause.

Today, however, they were back in a drab waiting room, looking over Robbie's shoulder at a poem she was reading aloud. The trick was to read it just loud enough so everyone in the room would have to listen and, hopefully, laugh.

Generally speaking, an oncology waiting room is not a particularly joyful place.

"OK," Robbie said, and she stood up to read. In order to see, the other three stood up with her. "This is the Mammogram Poem from the internet. I got it in an email and, as far as I can tell, there's no copyright or anything that says we can't read it aloud."

Total quiet.

Robbie held the tablet in front of her and began to read. Marge placed her hand over her heart and Hadley and Mary Rose did the same and looked serious.

> For years and years they told me,
> Be careful of your breasts.
> Don't ever squeeze or bruise them.
> And give them monthly tests.

So I heeded all their warnings,
And protected them by law.
Guarded them very carefully,
And I always wore my bra.
After 30 years of astute care,
My gyno, Dr. Pruitt,
Said I should get a Mammogram.
"O.K," I said, "let's do it."
"Stand up here real close," she said,
(She got my boob in line,)
"And tell me when it hurts," she said,
"Ah yes! Right there, that's fine."
She stepped upon a pedal,
I could not believe my eyes!
A plastic plate came slamming down,
My hooter's in a vice!
My skin was stretched and mangled,
From underneath my chin.
My poor boob was being squashed,
To Swedish Pancake thin.
Excruciating pain I felt,
Within its vice-like grip.
A prisoner in this vicious thing,
My poor defenseless tit!
"Take a deep breath," she said to me,
Who does she think she's kidding?!?
My chest is mashed in her machine,
And woozy I am getting.
"There, that's good," I heard her say,
(The room was slowly swaying.)

"Now, let's have a go at the other one."
Have mercy, I was praying.
It squeezed me from both up and down,
It squeezed me from both sides.
I'll bet SHE'S never had this done,
To HER tender little hide.
Next time that they make me do this,
I will request a blindfold.
I have no wish to see again,
My knockers getting steamrolled.
If I had no problem when I came in,
I surely have one now.
If there had been a cyst in there,
It would have gone "ker-pow!"
This machine was created by a man,
Of this, I have no doubt.
I'd like to stick his balls in there,
And see how THEY come out.

The waiting room, made up entirely of women, broke into applause and began to talk to each other, side by side, about their own mammograms and surgeries.

A sisterhood was formed.

In order to prevent further reading, Mary Rose was taken into the examining room in record time. The other three followed.

"I'm sorry," the nurse whose name tag actually read "Nurse Hurt, R", said "but only one person is allowed in at a time."

The others went back to the boring beige waiting room.

"Rev up your tablet, Robbie," Marge said, an angry tone in her voice. "Go to iTunes and find the Hokey Pokey. Let's see how many of these ladies like to dance."

In just a few minutes, the good Doctor Weaks appeared in Mary Rose's room. He smiled at Mary Rose's chart – not at Mary Rose – and opened his mouth. It was then that music came crashing through the door.

"You put your left foot in,
Your left foot out,
Your left foot in
And you shake it all about
You do the Hokey Pokey
And turn yourself around."

"What the hell is that?" Doctor Weaks asked.

He still hadn't made eye contact or looked at Mary Rose, so he didn't see her smile and shrug innocently.

Mary Rose McGill, model patient.

Knees of my Bees (Alanis Morissette, 2004)

They were walking down the long, dismal hall toward Marge's orthopedic physician, known simply as her "ortho."

"Billy Joel, George and Barbara Bush, Ray Charles, Steven Tyler, Lionel Richie, Katharine Hepburn, Elizabeth Taylor, Arnold Schwarzenegger, Michael Douglas, Liza Minnelli, Jane Fonda." Marge recited the list without taking a breath.

"You didn't even use commas in that sentence," Robbie said.

They were puffing just a little, keeping up with Marge and her red cane.

"It took me awhile to memorize it," she said.

"All those people who are famous and who had joints replaced," Mary Rose said, a touch of wonder in her voice.

It's like a list of breast enlargement patients," Hadley said. "It just goes on and on."

They came to the door of the doctor's office. Marge opened it and went in first.

This time, they just sat. They each picked up a magazine, most of them old ones, from a cheap brown table in the center of the room. They watched the other people in the waiting room, some dozing, some talking, younger people accompanying older people – a caregiver here, a caregiver there.

The chairs were straight and uncomfortable. The silence screamed at them. People talked in lowered voices. They looked at each other and did eyerolls and shrugs. They looked at watches and smart phones. They sighed.

The BOOB Girls. Real party animals.

Finally Marge was called into an examining room. They followed her in. The doctor came in fifteen minutes later. He didn't seem to notice them. He basically brutalized Marge's knee and said he'd see her in a year.

She asked about it hurting a lot.

He said she could have pain pills if she wanted.

She declined.

They left.

"One time," Marge said on the way out, "I had just showered and put on my bathrobe. My hair was wet.

I wiggled into that awful elastic stocking and my knee started to itch like crazy. I put my hand into the stocking to scratch the itch and my ring caught on the damn thing. I couldn't get my hand out, I couldn't get off the bed where I was sitting, I couldn't move. I finally reached my cell phone and called Omaha's best B & E man."

"Breaking and Entering," Mary Rose said.

"Right. And he came. Got through three dead bolts on my door in about twenty seconds, poured himself coffee as he came through my kitchen, flipped out his switchblade and cut off my stocking without saying a word. Then he left with his coffee in my favorite mug."

"Criminal!" Robbie said, shaking her head.

Hadley did an eyeroll.

"Why are all the waiting rooms so drab and ugly?" Mary Rose asked as they sat at Table 12 that evening. The other diners had gone back to their apartments.

Geoffrey was asleep beneath the table and Chaos had joined them, as usual.

"There is no color there," Hadley added. "What if one wall was bright yellow and another tasteful orange, then some blues and greens added."

"What if the chairs were cushioned and comfortable?" Robbie sked.

"What if there was good music or each chair had earphones so every patient could listen to their own music or news or whatever?" Mary Rose added.

"What if someone catered in some wine and cheese?" Marge suggested.

"You mean they don't have coffee bars?" Chaos asked.

"You jest, my dear," Robbie said.

"Darn!" Chaos said.

"Why don't they have a comedian come in once in awhile?" Mary Rose asked.

"They did," Robbie said, "it was us."

"I think doctors offices actually make you feel worse," Hadley said. "They aren't cozy or comfortable. And let's face it. Even the single patient hospital room is dull and drab and has machinery out in plain sight. They could redesign those and make them much nicer."

"They could have a building with an atrium and live piano music and people could get coffee and drinks and there would be new magazines and books and all kinds of good things in a bright and cheery atmosphere, like that new experiment in Omaha," Hadley said.

Unfortunately, none of them could remember the name of the new experiment that tried to make waiting for the doctor a pleasant experience, not a boring, anxiety-filled ordeal.

"It all needs to be remodeled," Hadley continued, "from the doctors' offices to the hospital rooms. It's time for the medical profession to come into the twenty-first century."

They nodded in agreement.

Part Three

The Girls: The Back Story

The fog comes in
On little cat feet.
It sits looking
Over harbor and city
On silent haunches
And then moves on.

Carl Sandburg

Our history laughs at us through cracked lips,
Smiles under bushy eyebrows and
Grins a snaggle-toothed grin at us.
That's our past, all right.
And we grow up and know to

Never Underestimate A Burned Out Old Broad

When You Gotta Go, You Gotta Go

It was just comfortable and cozy. Spring was beginning to peek around the big trees of Meadow Lakes and little daffodils were popping up out of the ground. The massive snow melt had soaked into the ground, leaving green grass and early blooms of crocus and snowbells.

The girls and animals were all in Hadley's apartment. Geoffrey was spread out at Mary Rose's feet with three white rats in sweaters nestled under his big, baggy chin. All four were sound asleep.

Hadley had made ice tea – the first of the season – and they were munching on cookies from Trader Joe's.

Chaos was getting a head start on the season and was wearing a short-sleeved T-shirt with a snake on it. It almost matched the big snake tattoo crawling up her arm. By now, they were all used to Chaos and the snake, they just hadn't seen it much through all the winter clothes.

Chaos took a deep breath.

"I'm leaving on Saturday," she announced.

They looked at her.

"I stayed a lot longer than I meant to," she continued. "You four have been such good friends. Darn! Every woman should have a Table 12."

She sighed.

They wondered if she was going to cry. Instead, she smiled.

"But I want to know about all of you. You know I grew up in New Orleans, had Marie Laveau for a role model. You don't know that both my parents were professors at the University of Louisiana."

They looked at her some more.

"Darn! Yep, I wasn't the first hippie in the family. They were war protesters, raging liberals, really fun people. There were parties at our house every week with students and teacher activists. I met some of the great civil right leaders like Harvey Milk and Jesse Jackson, and once, I actually met Dr. Martin Luther King, Jr. My folks both taught sociology."

She paused.

"I think you should know I have a doctorate in sociology, too."

They looked stunned.

"I know," she said, lowering her head and cocking it a little to one side. "Darn, it's hard to believe. I started out doing research on voodoo for an article for a journal and kind of got carried away."

"A doctorate?" Robbie squeaked.

"Yep. I make a good living freelancing with journals. In fact, I'm going to do a paper on the older woman – The Wise Woman in A Wicked World and take a look at the sociological aspects of aging and being unrecognized for who you are and what you do. Older women, like Mary Rose says, are beautiful."

"And you have white rats?" Mary Rose said. They all noticed that while Chaos looked the same, just telling them she was a PhD had allowed her voice to change, to become, well, more intelligent. She thought a little about Mary Rose's comment about Double-Double, Toil and Trouble.

"Love animals." She smiled. "I once played Lady Macbeth in college; that's where I got to love their names."

She looked at the girls and smiled. "So that's kind of my past. Our pasts are full of surprises and they make us who we are. I want to put your pasts in my paper, if it's okay with you and to do that, I want you to think about them. Like that little dude, Willie, said,

'You are your past. Your past is always with you.'" So how about we meet here on Friday and you tell me your stories?"

"Not an exact quote from Willie, Chaos, but close enough," Hadley smiled and took a sip of her tea. Geoffrey stretched, pushing Toil at least a foot away from his cozy spot. Toil gave the big dog a dirty look and scurried back, snuggling in even closer.

"A doctorate!" Robbie squeaked again. Then she looked at Chaos, "Darn!" she said with a wide smile.

Marge
The Laundromat

The past is always with you.
The past is always you.
It looks at us through bushy eyebrows
And a snaggle-toothed smile.

It was true. The past changed some as you grew old,
but it was always there, like the ugly little birthmark
on her neck that she could usually hide under a collar
or with a scarf. Ugly. Sad. Out of place. Weren't good
people supposed to have good pasts? Her mother had
said so. Her mother was usually wrong.

Marge muttered an "ummph," and, standing on the
crumbling sidewalk, looked through the window of
the old laundromat. The lone customer was a college
student folding his clothes into a laundry basket, his
backpack on the floor by the window.

Her mother was a raging paranoid schizophrenic.
Even the voices that whispered in her head could not
be depended upon. They lied. Just like her father.

The laundromat. It was run down. At one time it had
been called Duds in Suds with Dogs. The owners had
actually sold hotdogs from the back room where they
had a little kitchen. Almost every time she was there,
the old lady who watched over the place slipped her a
hotdog.

Thinking of it made her mouth water.

Marge went inside. It smelled of mold and damp more than detergent and bleach like it had when she had been a girl here on Leavenworth Street. Then it had been big. And clean. And safe.

Oh yes, they were industrial-sized memories that flooded in.

> The past is always with you.
> The past is always you.

.

They showed up crystal clear through the newly-cleaned eyeglasses of recollection or like the rearview mirror that had been adjusted correctly. Like the old song, she could see clearly now, the pain was gone. Or was it rain that was gone? Either way, Marge Aaron had walked into her past as surely as her foot had stepped over the rusted threshold and through that dingy, dirty door.

Somewhere in the background a motor was running, heat or air conditioning probably. Whatever it was, it was losing the war. "Homeless. Homeless. Homeless," it growled out in an off-key rhythm. Marge Aaron had been a homeless teenager. She had been a runaway. She had survived and had only told three people about her youth on the streets; her husband, her son and her daughter. But those years had made her street smart. They had made her a damned good cop.

Homeless.

Marge's memory settled into a city park. Now
the park was in a trendy area. The new Midtown
Crossing had made it beautiful and upscale. Years
ago, she and her mother had pretty much lived in
that park, then walked the several blocks to the
laundromat - when they had quarters and when there
was enough laundry to do. Eight people who lived in
the park, not even knowing each other's real names,
threw all their dirty clothes into a garbage bag and
chipped in with the quarters. Marge was fifteen. She
did the laundry. One time she had laundered Beagle
the Eagle and was afraid he would fall apart, but he
survived.

Beagle the Eagle was a hand puppet, a beautiful,
protective bird that fit over her fingers so she could
flap his long eagle wings, who could kiss her with
his beak, who would protect her, although with her
mother and seven grown, polite, homeless men, she
was pretty well protected. And what did she need
protecting from, anyway…the future?

Beagle the Eagle had lain flat in the bottom of her
backpack. Now, Beagle the Eagle lay flat in the
bottom of her nightgown drawer at Meadow Lakes.
Sometimes, when she couldn't sleep at night, she
took him out, put him on her hand and talked to him.
Beagle was an excellent listener. He bent his head

and folded his wings around her wrist and didn't say a word. Then he would kiss her cheek as gently as ever her husband could do.

Good old Beagle.

And he never complained about all the other stuff that was shoved into the backpack. They had found the backpack beside one of those big bins where people put clothes for poor people. Someone had liked the backpack and hadn't just thrown it into the big clothes box. It was laid carefully beside the bin, waiting to be noticed for the fine pack it was. It was dark blue, a good strong fabric with real leather straps and it held everything young Margie Aaron owned in the world.

She went over the inventory in her head:
Two shirts (one red, one green – her own Christmas colors right there on her back.

Light jacket she had rolled tight (green plastic)
A roll of quarters (sometimes she got to play pinball machines.)

Comb (She pulled all the hair out of it every day.)
A half roll of toilet paper (useful for many things)
Mouthwash (stolen from the Blackstone Hotel on south 36th Street.)

For a few minutes, Margie was back at the Blackstone with all its elegance. She still loved it. Back then, she would wait until after school, when she went to school, then walk into the Blackstone with her backpack strapped over her shoulders and her hair in a ponytail. She strode in like she owned the place. "Act like you know what you're doing and everyone will believe you do." That's what her speech teacher told them and it was true. Sneak around and someone will catch you and ask questions, but just walk in like you know where you're going and you're home free.

It didn't hurt that Louis, the doorman, in his red coat and red top hat knew her and liked her. She always smiled at him. Now and then, when it was way too hot to be dressed in a red coat and red top hat – not to mention the boots that came halfway up his black slacks - she went inside, got cold water in her plastic cup from the backpack and took it out to him.

Margie the kid, whom her homeless crowd called "Kiddo," would walk casually down the long corridors of the big hotel until she found a housekeeping cart parked in front of a guestroom and the cleaning lady working inside. It was always safer if she could hear a vacuum humming away inside the room. Margie would look around – again, casually – then grab what she could from the cart, so in her backpack were also those little soaps, shampoo (she never bothered with the conditioner) and lots of mouthwash. You couldn't keep a toothbrush clean in a filled-up backpack, so she cleaned her teeth religiously with mouthwash.

Her memories came in waves. She hadn't thought this hard about the Blackstone in a long time, but every time she drove by it, triggers went off, just like her revolver on the firing range. Bang! Bang! Bang! Flashes of pictures in her mind like the flashes from her gun when she fired it.

One summer she had lived under the Blackstone for two weeks. There was a back entrance where coal used to be loaded into the old hotel, and Margie had stolen a pillow and slept just in front of the door that was well-hidden by an overhang and small walls on either side of the entrance. Two weeks. She was alone then. Her mother had been taken away in handcuffs, Margie wasn't sure why, but when she saw the police head toward her raging mother, she had backed quietly into the alley behind the police car and pressed herself into the shadows of the wall.

Social Services were not her friends.

She sat down carefully in one of the cheap white plastic chairs by the windows of the laundromat. The college student hurried out the door, his folding done, not looking her way. She was an old lady now. Invisible.

She didn't know if she had kept her time on the street a secret or if she just hadn't taken the time to talk about it with her three best friends. She had come close once.

Hadley had looked at her and just making friendly conversation, asked, "What did your father do, Marge?"

"Go away." She had smiled.

"And your mother, what did she do?"

"Go crazy."

Then, either Mary Rose or Robbie had interrupted with something about somebody at Meadow Lakes and they had never spoken of it again.

> A feeling shared is a feeling diminished.
> A secret shared is a secret destroyed.

She went back to her mental inventory of her backpack:

Three used detective paperbacks. One Frisbee. (She didn't play Frisbee, but when something was free, you took it no matter what it was or how useful it could be.)

One plastic cup (the one she used when she got water for Louis the doorman) and that she used to pour water over her hair when she could wash it.
An "I like Ike" button she had found in the grass.

There was no underwear. She never wore underwear. Somewhere deep in her brain she still wondered if wearing underwear was all that healthy. All it did was keep your clothes clean. She wore it now. She even liked some of it.

There was more in her backpack, but it was stuff that came and went. Usually, when she went to school, it was so full that she carried her schoolbooks while the other kids put theirs in the backpacks from Scheels or Dick's Sporting Goods.

She struggled to her feet and held her cane like a gun, pointing it all around the laundromat. She walked over to the counter that had held the hotdogs, turned and leaned on it, getting a new perspective on the room, just like she was getting a new perspective on life.

The hotdogs reminded her of eating at the Blackstone. She would walk through the fancy restaurant and pick up food and hide it under her shirt. She always ate well and she was making history. She was eating Reuben sandwiches and they had been created right there in that very restaurant by Reuben Kulakofsky, a grocer from Lithuania who played poker with the hotel owner.

Cool.

She didn't eat Ruebens much anymore though.

Then she had gotten caught. There was a little store close to the Blackstone and the owner saw her snitch a loaf of bread. Marge had never considered it stealing, she considered it surviving. But this time the police showed up. Marge had read about Mary Bryant, the young girl from the eighteenth century who was convicted of stealing a petticoat and ended up on a prison ship headed for Australia. A petticoat. High class homeless there. The Reubens were equally big time for Marge.

She took one more look around the old laundromat and walked slowly to the door. Her hand lingered on the old glass knob. She took one last look.

> The past is always with you.
> The past is always you.

She somehow felt friendlier toward the old laundromat. It had aged along with her, but she had aged better. And, by God, she had used her past to, you might say, get past it.

Past your past.

She chuckled under her breath and walked toward the Hummer.

One more stop to make.

Turner Park

Not what it used to be, that's for sure. There were probably still a few "ladies of the night," as her mother called them, who worked the park or near it. The prostitutes had always been nice to Marge. She counted on them for her candy supply and once in a while they gave her things like lipstick and barrettes for her hair.

She parked along the street, got out of the Hummer and walked to a park bench and sat down facing the beautiful old Clarinda and Page apartment building. She had lived in this park. It hadn't been such a bad home.

How things change! That loaf of bread had skyrocketed her into a new life. The only telephone number the police could associate with Marge had been an aunt and uncle she had only met once, way back when, before her mother joined the looney crowd one hundred percent.

At first, they didn't want to come or to claim her. She had felt like a lost dog no one wanted. But they had changed their minds and not only shown up, they gave her a home and sent her to school. She had no school records and no health records, but the school gave her this test – something from Iowa and she did the equivalent of what today would be scoring one hundred percent on an SAT exam.

Standardized Achievement Test. Well, she had achieved, all right.

The National Merit Scholarship had just been created and Marge merited her way right into college, then right into the Army and directly into the Military Police.

The rest was history.

> The past is always with you.
> The past is always you.

Marge sat on the bench for a while, the breeze gently moving the leaves in the many trees that shaded the park. Ominous, roiling storm clouds were gathering in the southwest. Distant lightning made a threat toward the sun that was still shining on Marge.

As the shadows chased the birds across the lush green grass, Marge Aaron smiled to herself, got up slowly and walked, her red cane over her arm, to the Hummer. She had another quote she liked better than the one about your past.

It is what it is.
It becomes what you make of it.

Robbie
The Album

The past is always with you.
The past is always you.

The storm outside was doing its thing. Lightning made a silent scream across the sky followed by a long, ominous growl of thunder that went on for several seconds. Rain pounded and roared against the windows. "God is bowling," her aunt used to say when it thundered. A second forked bolt of lightning shot across the sky and legions of thunder marched toward the river. The rain pounded harder.

Robinson Leary had stuck a cup of cold coffee into the microwave and when the little chime rang to tell her it was hot, she grabbed the cup, picked up her reading glasses from the table and headed for her couch.

The lightning lit up her apartment like a flashbulb. Setting her cup and glasses on the little table next to the couch, Robbie took a few steps to the wall next to the couch and once again opened the small hutch her father had made for her when she was three years old.

Two doors in the bottom revealed stacks of albums and books. Robbie looked for a second, then pulled one out that lay close to the bottom. It was big and thick, probably 15x18 inches, designed to hold photos and documents. Yellow edges of newspaper clippings stuck out of the top and bottom.

Robbie took the album to the couch and sat down, kicking off her shoes and curling her feet to one side in her favorite sitting position. The lightning flashed again and the thunder rumbled louder this time. It was a perfect setting for what she was going to do – something she had refused to do for nearly two decades.

She was going to really read what was in the album.

The first page was a large copy of a portrait, that of a beautiful woman of color. It was claimed, although Robbie doubted it, that this was her great, or was it great-great grandmother. She would have to write down dates and count backward to make sure because some of the names in the album had been torn out or lost.

The woman in the picture was extremely striking and haunting. Robbie had seen the portrait, actually had been forced to view it, in a museum in New Orleans years ago. She was twelve and an aunt from Brooklyn had come with the hidden agenda to teach her niece the family history.

Robinson Leary, even at that young age, didn't want to learn.

"Look at her!" Aunt Philomene had said in a coarse whisper,while pointing an arthritis-twisted finger toward a nearly life-sized portrait hanging on the wall.

"Look at her!"

Robbie had looked.

It was a beautiful portrait of the beautiful woman.

"See those cheekbones, those eyes, that hair. That is YOU, child! That is you."

Aunt Philomene spoke loudly and never let go of Robbie's arm. She was holding it so tight it hurt. Robbie was looking, but she didn't see the cheekbones or the eyes. She saw the yellow turban, the red shawl and the hands holding a live chicken that was standing still on some circular disc with what looked to Robbie like a hex symbol. She saw the bottles and bags of herbs and potions, a frightening and frightened-looking little black figurine kneeling on the table at which the woman sat. On shelves behind her were more figurines, frightening; even though they, too, were small.

Young Robbie shivered involuntarily.

"Look at her face, child," Aunt Philomene whispered. "Look at her face."

Today, in Robbie's apartment, the lightning from the storm lit up the woman's face as if it followed the commands of Aunt Philomene. Memories of that day in the museum flashed along with the lightning. Robbie looked again at the woman in the album.

She was one of the most beautiful women Robinson Leary had ever seen. Yes, those were Robbie's eyes, all right; she was the same build as the woman in the portrait. This woman, though, was darker, her skin reflecting in the flashes of lightning. In a strange way she seemed to be looking right at Robbie, just as she did that day when Aunt Philomene had introduced them.

Robinson Leary was looking into the eyes of a possible ancestor. Robinson Leary, a small smile dimpling her cheeks, was looking into the eyes of the famous Marie Laveau, the voodoo queen of New Orleans; Marie Laveau, upon whose grave offerings were still placed, even today, requesting the magic of the greatest voodoo priestess of all time.

Robbie turned the page and read the inscription – the only thing on the entire page:

To my niece, Robinson Jean Christophe Dominica Leary

No one knew her full name except her late husband and the government.

Robbie sipped her coffee and looked out at the storm. Thinking how all her adult life perhaps, she had lived a lie. It had started in junior high when they began to study Louisiana history. She had said her ancestry was Cajun. Who didn't love Longfellow's Evangeline?

Still stands the forest primeval; but far away from its shadow, side by side, in their nameless graves, the lovers are sleeping.

But she could claim the Cajun ancestry through only one great-great aunt. The truth was, she was probably Creole, and Creole in her growing up years meant one thing – voodoo. Dark-skinned Creole kids were shunned in the areas of New Orleans where she grew up.

The shadow-haunted apartment darkened in the storm. Robbie reached up, unconsciously, and pulled the tiny chain to turn on the lamp on the table by the couch, her eyes never leaving those of Marie Laveau.

There had been songs written and sung about the voodoo queen, most of them very uncomplimentary, some so beautiful and jazz-filled they brought tears to Robbie's eyes when she had listened to them on YouTube a few years ago.

The windows were streaming with rain now. Robbie leafed through the album for more pictures and she wasn't disappointed. Men had wanted to paint Marie Laveau's portrait. Some were exotic. Many included her one-eyed snake, Zombi.

Robbie couldn't tell if Zombi was a cobra or a python or some other kind of creature, but he was huge and heavy as he wound around Marie's waist, her shoulders and her neck.

Robbie looked up and watched the rain pour down outside and onto the windows.

She had never been afraid of snakes. Oh, she had screamed when other girls screamed, even with her three friends here at Meadow Lakes, but she found snakes comforting and thought they felt like expensive silk.

She could relate to the woman holding this gorgeous reptile.

It was said her supposedly great-great grandmother had a one-eyed snake and a three legged dog. Robbie found no pictures of the dog. In a way, she hoped she actually was related to the notorious priestess.

There were things Robinson Jean Christophe Dominica Leary had never told anyone, though her strange aunt, Philomene, would have loved knowing. Robinson somehow knew things she shouldn't know. She knew, for example, that she should move to Meadow Lakes and the words "Four Friends" kept coming into her mind all the time she was moving.

She knew Mary Rose McGill would meet Wiley Vondra. She knew when Alphonso Greatwood rolled through the door for the first time, even though she was in her apartment when he entered the building. Robinson Leary knew Wes Longbow was dead before Hadley sent the text to meet her. And she knew something bad was going to happen to one of them, and soon. She had learned to always, without exception, trust these visions, trust her intuition.

There was another clap of thunder, directly overhead, in rhythm to Robbie's turning the page.

She smiled.

If people thought Robinson Jean Christophe Dominica Leary's name was strange, wait till they met her father's side of the family, headed, back in the voodoo queen's time, by none other than Dr. Yah Yah.

No wonder Robbie had a thing about funny names.

She owned a bunch of them.

Dr. Yah Yah was a Haitian slave, well known for his potions and healing powers. Robbie looked at a drawing of him – big, strong, black as night. He was famous and, after he gave a rich client a potion that contained a deadly poison, he became even more famous. Was he hung? Robbie couldn't remember and couldn't find it in the album.

She thought for a minute. She remembered her father talking about him once and laughing about Yah Yah training zombes. zombes, named after the Haitian God, Nzambi. How in the world do you train a zombie? And she wasn't talking about Marie's snake.

She smiled.

And there was something else. She, Robinson, had learned to call her grandmother Mambo, an old Creole name that went back hundreds of years.

The storm was growing weaker. The thunder was far away now, the rain reduced to a steady drizzle. Robbie's coffee had grown cold.

She shut the album.

She knew about her father. He had named her after Jackie Robinson, who broke the Black barrier in baseball. Good old #42. He had been safe for her to study. No snakes or voodoo priests around old Jackie. But her father hadn't known Jackie in the big leagues, when he was hired by the Dodgers and got death threats every day.

Oh, no, her father knew him when they both played for a season in the Negro League. Even then, Jackie could run faster than the wind and, so the story goes, drug her father, drunk, out of a bar and, as Daddy used to say, "Beat the crap out of me." Her father never drank again and credited Robinson with saving his life and career.

Her father became an attorney.

Robinson became a professor.

She closed the album.

Enough.

She didn't want to be a descendant of voodoo priests and priestesses. She wanted to be herself, here at Meadow Lakes Retirement Community, living a good life and surrounded by the best friends anyone could have.

The past is always with you.
The past is always you.

She got up, rinsed out her cup and put it in the cupboard. She put the album back into the hutch and looked out the window. The sky was still dark. Dusk was climbing down through the trees. A small, lone bat flew in its jagged flight toward one of the security lights that had just come on.

It was time for dinner. Robbie opened her door and started down the hall toward the dining room and Table 12. As she closed the door, she looked at the sign hanging on it.

She believed she could do it
So she did.

Robinson Jean Christophe Dominica had done it. She was Doctor Leary and had not had to cast one voodoo spell to get there.

God bless Chaos Cauldron.

Hadley
The Little Heart

Hadley Joy Morris-Whitfield was walking down the long, cool corridors of Meadow Lakes. One hand kept going into the pocket of her slacks.

> The past is always with you.
> The past is always you.

Her fingers found the tiny little heart she almost always carried with her. It had been the last gift from her father the year he died, decades ago now.

Every Christmas her dad had gotten Hadley and her mother White Shoulders perfume for Christmas; not cologne, not toilet water, real perfume. Several years ago, before she came to the retirement community, Hadley had squirted White Shoulders on her wrists in a drug store. It used to be sold only in department stores – much too nice for regular drug stores – until more expensive scents had chased it into relative affordability.

She was amazed that she could ever have worn such a scent. It was way too floral, way too strong. But when her Dad had given it to her, it was precious and just what she wanted. She wore it on every date in high school and had taken it to college with her. During that last year, the year of her father's death, the little heart-shaped bottle had come with a tiny metal heart attached. Hadley had loved it. Now it was old and scarred, the gold worn off, there was a scratch all across the front.

Her father had been a letter carrier. At that time in postal history, he was called a mailman. And he loved Hadley Joy. He loved her a little too much, not in a sexual way at all, but more than he loved her mother.

And her mother didn't much love Hadley Joy at all.

"Hadley Joy, my boy!" her father called her when he was joking with her, but her being a girl was no joke.

It was almost an affront to her mother.

Hadley had been born twenty years after a sister she would never know died at age three of pneumonia. Rowena. Hadley knew her name, knew her story. Knew how she had reached her thin little arms up toward the ceiling as she was dying and said, "Look, Mommy, look! See the babies. See all the babies!"

It had been a great comfort to her mother. The minister had said it meant she was seeing angels coming to take her young soul. Hadley believed it, too, a good way for a child to die, if a child had to die.

There were no baby angels in the sky today; just scars of lightning and timpani of thunder.

After the untimely death of Rowena, her mother decided not to have any more children. How had they worked that, Hadley wondered. There was no birth control back in those days. Had her mother, even then, in her twenties, refused to have sex with her father? He was a handsome man. He met Robbie's criteria for a relationship – Big, Strong, Tall, Handsome and Intelligent. But there hadn't been any other children until her mother found herself pregnant with Hadley at age forty.

"We were so surprised," a cousin told her once. "Of course, she was long over Rowena's death."

Oh, no, she wasn't. She wasn't over it at all.

One aunt liked to play an emotional game Hadley learned was called, "Let's you and her fight." She drove wedges between people, hoping to make them mad at each other so she could be the one most liked.

When Hadley was a teenager, her aunt had told her, "You know, when your mother knew you were on the way, she said, 'At least I won't have to have another little girl.'"

She had laughed a friendly, loving laugh and

smoothed Hadley's hair with her hand, as if she were cementing the wedge she had just driven between mother and daughter.

"Hadley Joy, my boy!"

She rubbed the heart that had become warm from being held in her hand.

Her mother seldom touched her, never hugged her. Her mother was needy. She expected to be taken care of. She was the quintessential housewife who did everything she was supposed to do - except be happy.

"If they could just give me something for my nerves!" her mother would say over and over. The doctor gave her tranquilizers, blood pressure pills, other "nerve medicine." Mother woke up every morning with a drug hangover which made her sicker and sicker.

"Be as quiet as you can, Hadley," her father would whisper. "Mommy has a sick headache."

Migraines – every few days it seemed.

And only Dad called his wife "Mommy." Hadley had called her "Mother" from the time she could say the word. "Mom," now and then, but mostly "Mother." And Daddy became Dad soon, too. It made her feel older, more in control of her life.

Her mother had never been mean to her, just never really noticed her.

In fact, her mother showed tremendous kindness about Hadley's thumb sucking. She remembered people telling her mother to put iodine on her thumb, to bandage her thumb, to put all kinds of evil sounding remedies on her thumb, but her mother just listened and nodded and never did anything to her hand. It was the first time Hadley knew what a feeling of gratitude and relief was.

She was carrying the little heart in her hand now, outside her pants pocket, all the way to the end of the long, long corridor where the downpour drenched the window and overflowed the drainpipe.

Never been mean to her.

But once, Hadley had really been afraid. Her father found her in a lawn chair, reading, in their back yard. She had been only nine or ten. "Hadley," he had said, leaning down over the lawn chair and taking hold of her shoulder. "Your mother is going through 'the change.' If she ever starts chasing you with a knife, you run just as fast as you can."

Then what?

Where should she run to?

He had turned and gone back into the house as if
he had announced they were having hamburger
and mashed potatoes for supper. Hadley had gone
to the library and looked up "The Change." After
some serious searching, she finally found it meant
menopause. She read about it.

Hadley had walked the entire third floor corridor of
Meadow Lakes and was starting on the second floor.
Her calves felt as if they might cramp.

> The past is always with you.
> The past is always you.

She remembered when her own periods had started.
Her mother hated things like that. She never talked
to Hadley about "woman troubles." Puberty came as
a total surprise. She went to the bathroom and her
panties were bloody. She called her mother into their
tiny little half bath off the kitchen, "Mom! Help!"
And Mom had come running. Her father was in
the bedroom next to the kitchen, sitting on the bed
changing his shoes. Her mother grabbed her bloody
panties and Hadley watched as she held them up for
her father to see.

Like it was his fault she was growing up.

Mother just stared at her father and shook her head
like it was a terrible thing. A few minutes later, she

came back into the tiny bathroom with a clean pair of panties and a belt and a feminine napkin. "This will happen every month now."

That was all her mother said. Hadley headed for the library again. "Menstruation." Other girls had talked about it. "Periods." But Hadley had never had friends with whom she could talk about such things. Her best friend was the library three blocks away in their small Nebraska town.

So much went on in that small town. Everybody knew everybody else. One lady had said, "The best thing about a small town is everybody knows you and knows your business. The worst thing about a small town is everybody knows you and knows your business."

Dean had told her his father hit his mother.

Gary had told her his father stole from his business.

Beth had told her a girl had cheated on a test to get into the band.

And there were all the scary stories about Dirty Neck Johnson, who wasn't quite right in the head and was to be avoided at all costs.

And in high school, there were all the girls who got

pregnant and "went away." Sherry, Kaye, Louise, Joan. The boys never seemed to care.

Hadley sat down for a few minutes in a big chair in the Meadow Lakes lobby.

Outside, the lightning flashed and the thunder sounded like a giant wheel moving over the city. She glanced out the window. Sheets of rain were washing against it as if it wanted to be invited in like some soaked vampire. She looked at the little heart.

Her father had carried a tiny cross in his pocket and pulled it out every time he reached for change. It was to remind him to think about whether or not he needed what he was planning to buy, or if the money would best be given to the church.

Her father was a good churchman.

Her mother never went.

Hadley didn't have a tiny cross. She had the little heart. She got up, sighed and started off on her walk once more.

Age twelve. That had been the time. Hadley read once that around age twelve children either consciously or unconsciously make a decision about what their lives will be. It was spot on for her.

Age twelve.

She was swinging in the porch swing on her front porch, one of her favorite places. Her dog, Skippy – she had gotten the name off the peanut butter jar – was in the swing beside her and she was doing what she always did, reading.

But Hadley Joy Morris wasn't reading Nancy Drew or the Hardy Boys or any of the other books kids her age read. Hadley Joy Morris was on a mission, a mission to be somebody, to be liked, to be part of something exciting. Being an only child can be lonely. Hadley Joy Morris was reading *How to Win Friends and Influence People.* Hadley was reading it because she didn't have any friends and couldn't influence anybody. Dale Carnegie, himself, had written it and it was easy to understand.

It had been a hassle to get it from the librarian, even though Hadley was well known. Back then, you had to read only the books listed for your age and for Hadley, twelve-year-olds read really boring stuff. She had told just a little fib.

"This is the book my mother wants, Mrs. Rambo. She said you could check it out on her card."

"Why would your mother want a book like that, Hadley?"

"She has to give a report for her book club. You can call her if you need to verify it."

"Verify"– a new word Hadley had memorized. She knew it would come in handy sometime.

It did.

"That won't be necessary, dear. I'm sure your mother will give a very good report."

Sure she would.

Hadley had hurried home and started reading right away. Three days later, she was ready for action.

At that age, Hadley was quite overweight, tall for her age and plain, plain, plain. She finished reading the book, stood up, patted Skippy on the head and headed back to the library. She even remembered what she wore that day; that day the library changed her life.

She checked out every book they had on beauty. There was no such thing as a book on fitness back then. "Fitness" wasn't even a word yet. This time the librarian didn't even question her. Must be Dale Carnegie liked beauty.

She changed how she ate. She didn't know anything about running – no one in town ran and "jogging" wasn't in the language either. She ran up and down the stairs leading to their bedrooms. She did jumping jacks and every exercise in the books. She got a new hairstyle. She read about and spent her allowance on makeup.

Young Hadley Joy was reinventing herself.

And it had worked.

Hadley opened the door to the stairway leading to her floor at Meadow Lakes and began to climb those stairs in honor of the stairs that had helped her lose weight and tone her legs years ago.

She smiled. She had subscribed to Seventeen Magazine and learned the tricks of the trade: *How to Make Boys Like You* (act like you're dumber than they are,) *Best Kept Secrets of the Stars* (use a lipstick brush). Hadley still had hers and by god she still used it), *Preparing for the Big Date* (it all started with a soak in a bubble bath).

By the end of the school year, Hadley was winning friends and influencing people.

She was devouring self-help books, the newest thing on the market, and she was learning a lot about family dynamics.

She was improving with self-improvement.

Grown up Hadley sat down on the top step leading to her floor. The building had shut out the storm and quieted it. This was the same step she had chosen when she waited to hear that Wes Longbow had died. She began to think. What did all this stuff from her past mean to her son? He was an only child as well. Hadley's mother had loved him, doted on him. Finally, the boy she wanted.

Hadley remembered the hurt she had felt when her mother was diagnosed with macular degeneration and said something to her. The little grandson was five or six and Mother had told Hadley, "Watch out for that little boy's eyes, Hadley. You take good care of them."

What about my eyes? Hadley had thought. What about mine? I'm next in line for the damn stuff.

Now, indeed, she had macular degeneration. One more gift from good old Mom. But Hadley's attitude was different. "For me," she told people, "ARMD stands for Armed and Dangerous, not Age-Related Macular Degeneration."

But had her relationships had anything to do with her son's four marriages? "The unhealthiest thing he eats is wedding cake," she had joked. But she and his father had a good marriage, even if a couple of affairs slithered in on it.

The past is always with you.
The past is always you.

She had loved high school. She achieved. She dated. She was a Homecoming Queen candidate. She went on to be the first person in her family to go to college.

She met her husband, who had been one of the rich frat boys. Hadley Joy Morris wanted more than anything to be rich and be loved. With this cute boy, she found both. She became Hadley Joy Morris-Whitfield, a name with a hyphen. She was lucky. "I am a lucky, happy woman," she said aloud.

"I didn't have it so bad. I used to not believe my parents did the best they could, but I believe it now. I am indeed, a lucky, happy woman." Hadley listened to the thunder and wondered if the storm thought it was a lucky, happy storm.

She had a sign, it seemed all four friends got each other little signs for doors or walls or shelves. Her favorite said:

You can blame your parents for how you turned out
But it's your fault if you choose to stay that way.

She didn't blame them anymore. She got up, opened the stairway door and walked toward her apartment. The window at the end of the hall was nearly black from the storm. Lightning lit up the hallway and elongated Hadley's shadow behind her, turning it into a ghostly phantom that followed her noiselessly through her door.

Mary Rose
The Golden Cross

The lightning was illuminating Mary Rose McGill's face as she looked out of the window. She was in her comfortable, red swivel rocking chair, facing the storm. She was clutching the little gold cross that hung on a gold chain around her neck. It was the most expensive piece of jewelry Mary Rose owned and she had just started wearing it. Now, she wore it nearly every day.

"Why tuck it away, Mary Rose?" Marge had asked. "You could grow old and die and never enjoy it."

That was true and Mary Rose was already old, old enough to decide to sit in her chair and pray instead of getting on her knees. Getting on your knees was okay, getting up was a bitch.

Her husband had given her the cross for a birthday years ago. He had been a very quiet man and a good provider. In looking at her life at Meadow Lakes, she realized that both he and she had been boring and dull.

Not anymore!

He was dead and she was a blond with red-rimmed glasses. Not to mention new pantsuits and a very cool, moderately long skirt or two – or three. She drank wine and, if they had dances at Meadow Lakes, Mary Rose McGill would have danced. She would have danced with Wiley Vondra and flirted and had fun. Wiley wasn't quiet. He was boisterous and loud and good.

Her husband had been a big change from her father and Wiley was a big change from her husband.

> The past is always with you.
> The past is always you.

Her father. The first memory that came as she held the little cross was of the Christmas tree. Hail Mary, full of grace. Mary Rose should have grabbed her rosary. Hail Mary, full of grace, the Lord is with thee. Mary Rose was saying the Hail Marys out loud, lifting her voice to the rain streaming down her double windows. Lightning seemed to punctuate her words, the thunder echoed her prayer.

Her father was an alcoholic, a good old Irish Catholic heavy drinker. That Christmas he had staggered home from the corner bar drunk as a skunk, however drunk skunks could get.

It was Christmas Eve and there were no presents under the tree. They would appear in the morning. Mary Rose knew there wasn't any Santa Claus, but the presents would appear while they slept. Clothes. Mittens. Boots. Socks. Maybe a new coat if she was lucky.

Blessed art thou among women. Her mother would put an orange, an apple and some uncracked nuts in the stockings they had hung. Mary Rose hated oranges and apples and nuts, but she and her two brothers had to pretend they were surprised and pleased.

Now, in her memory, she was sitting in a chair in her little Catholic school girl uniform. Her father, not noticing her, yelled at her mother to get in the F___ ing living room! Her mother had appeared from the kitchen wearing her usual apron and holding a dish towel.

Blessed also is the fruit of thy womb, Jesus.

 "That tree looks like shit, woman! Did the brats decorate it again?"

Her mother looked at Mary Rose and told her father to shut the F up! Her father didn't care. He took an off-center swing at her mother, lost his balance and fell headlong into the tree.

It was dry, as it always was, and brown needles went all over that side of the room. Ornaments broke. The lights pulled out of their sockets and went out. The tinsel, "icicycles" the family called them, looked like tiny silver worms thrown out of a bucket. A stream of curses came out of her father's mouth, matched by her mother's. Mary Rose slipped out of her chair and ran as fast as she could into her oldest brother's room.

Holy Mary, Mother of God, pray for us now and at the hour of our death.

Her oldest brother was ten years older than Mary Rose, and her mother's favorite. He was tall for his age, with the typical red hair and a great smile.

"Hey,Cozy Rosie, the old man scaring you again? You can stay here, just be quiet."

The door opened and her other brother slipped in. "It's gonna be bad," he said. "Real bad."

"Always is this time of year," oldest brother said.

Mary Rose climbed up onto her brother's bed, lay flat and put a pillow over her head.

Her mother loved her brothers, but not her. She was the one who caught all the criticism, who did everything wrong. Her mother had wanted three sons, like the television show, "My Three Sons."

Mary Rose knew if she only tried harder her mother would love her.

Her father didn't love anybody.

They had a dog once.

He had beaten it to death.

He had whipped his sons with his belt until their backs were raw.

And their mother didn't help them. It was as if she wanted the fight, she wanted to hurt him and she could hold her own in a knock-down, drag-out fight with him, then they would beat each other all the way into their bedroom and make scary noises that made her brothers shake their heads, but that Mary Rose didn't understand; loud noises and sometimes yells and screams and rattling of the bed. It was not a happy house for children.

Merry Christmas to all, and to all a good night.

The lightning seemed to be right outside Mary Rose's window. The lightning was her mother, the thunder her father.

She had grown up shy and scared.

Hail Mary full of grace.

She started aloud again, still holding the little cross.

The Lord is with thee.

She fully believed Blessed Mother Mary was with her the night her father had come home drunk and her mother wasn't there. Mary Rose couldn't remember where Mama had gone, it was so many years ago. But she remembered her father opening her bedroom door without knocking, leering at her, smelling of sweat and whiskey.

She had one year left in high school. Her oldest brother had gotten a big scholarship to Notre Dame and her other brother was in his room. He had graduated last year and was working at a Dairy Queen, featuring the new soft serve ice cream.

"Hello, pretty girl," her father was as drunk as she had ever seen him.

The Lord is with thee.

Mary Rose couldn't run from the room. He was between her and the door.

"Don't, Papa," she whispered. She was on her feet backing away. She didn't know what he was going to do, but his face was terrible, like he looked at her mother before he beat her. "Please don't, Papa."

Blessed art thou among women.

She was easing around him; he was working to keep his balance. "Come here, Mary Rose. Papa just wants a little kiss, just a little kiss from his little girl."

His words were slurred and terrible. He was unbuckling his belt and unzipping his dirty work trousers. "Just a little kiss."

Blessed also is the fruit of thy womb, Jesus.

"No, Papa!" Mary Rose yelled. She dived for the open door. As she ducked through, she went under the closed fist of her brother, the fist that connected to their father's nose and sent a spray of blood over the floor and onto her brother.

Her brother hit their father with his other fist: he moved back and caught the old man with a fierce blow under the chin. Her father staggered backward, surprised and trying to gain purchase on the wood floor to stay upright.

For the first time, Mary Rose noticed her brother was as tall and as big as their father.

Her brother followed Papa as he went backward, his fists repeating blow after blow to the head. Her father's eyes were already blackened and shut. He tried to grab hold of his son, but failed. Somehow, Mary Rose needed to do something, something she had actually imagined doing before.

Her father was on his knees, his head in his hands. Her brother was still delivering blows to the ears and the head of the man who had started it all.

Smash! Crack! Blow after blow after blow.

If they had been in a comic book, words like, "POW!! "SOCK!!" "WHAM!!" would have been over their heads.

Now her brother was kicking Papa.

Mary Rose picked up a large statue of the Virgin that Mama had made sure was in every bedroom. It was porcelain and heavy. Mary Rose grasped it in both hands, walked calmly to her brother, whose arm was pulled back, ready for another jab, touched him on the shoulder so he would know she was there and smashed the statue as hard as she could onto the top of her father's head.

Her father slumped to the floor, blood flowing from his nose, eyes, ears and the horrific gash the Virgin had delivered to him on the top of his head. The Virgin Mary shattered into a hundred pieces, her beautiful head rolling under Mary Rose's bed.

Brother and sister looked at each other. Her brother was breathing hard, so was Mary Rose. Her brother's face was covered with sweat, but there was no blood on him, except that of his father.

Mary Rose smiled.

Her brother smiled back.

"Thank you," she whispered.

"You're welcome," he said. He went to Mary Rose's little desk, got a piece of paper and one of her pens. He wrote a simple note.

If you ever touch her again
I will come back and kill you.

He grabbed one of the big oversized thumbtacks from Mary Rose's bulletin board, walked over to his father and stuck the thumbtack through the paper and into the old man's hand. A new stream of blood glistened out and ran past the tack and onto the floor.

Her brother stepped back and kicked his father in the ribs as hard as he could. His boots had metal toes.

Mary Rose was sure she could hear a rib crack.

Her brother held her for a moment, then kissed the top of her head. "I'll be watching," he whispered. He turned and walked out the door. In just minutes, Mary Rose saw him go out the front door with his duffle bag over his shoulder.

She never saw him again.

Pray for us now and at the hour of our death.

The memories were coming faster than the tears running down Mary Rose's cheeks. Mary Rose – before she was Mary Rose McGill, seemed to case herself in plastic as she stood over her unconscious father.

There were no words then for post traumatic stress syndrome, but Mary Rose was a prime candidate. She had just fought her own war.

She took hold of her father's foot and started dragging him across the wooden floor and out the door of her room. He was so heavy, a dead weight, and Mary Rose didn't know if he was dead or just unconscious. She didn't care. For the first time in her young life, she really didn't care. She dug in her heels and pulled. He was halfway out the door. She stepped over his middle and saw again the unzipped trousers.

She shivered. Then she got down on her knees and pushed against his shoulders with both hands.

He moved a little, leaving a small trail of blood beneath his head.

She pushed harder. She was sweating and grunting, a strange combination of grunting and little girl crying.

She pushed again, got up, stepped over his chest this time, grabbed him by both feet, faced away from him and pulled like a horse would pull a wagon.

He was in the hall.

Mary Rose turned and looked at him. He looked pitiful, wounded, a shameful mass of unmanliness. Mary Rose realized she was holding her breath. She let out a huge sigh, looked at him one more time and stepped carefully around him and headed for the bathroom at the end of the hall.

She thought of Lady Macbeth trying to wash out the spot of blood on her hands. They had just read it in literature class.

"Out, out, damned spot."

Mary Rose's damned spot went spinning down the drain. She splashed cold water on her face and looked in the little mirror over the sink. She looked older. Mary Rose knew she was older, older by a life experience that changed who she was.

She soaked a towel in the sink, wrung it out with her hands and went back to her room. On her hands and knees, she wiped up all the blood her father had left for her.

She went to her dresser and got her pink billfold with eight dollars in it. As she walked out of her room and into the hallway, where her father still lay motionless, she opened up the towel and covered his face with it. She smiled a little smile. "You look a lot better that way, Papa." And she went down the stairs, headed for the drugstore on the corner. Like so many old drugstores, this one had a fair line of hardware supplies. Mary Rose was looking for two big door hooks to lock her door, the kind that dropped into a ring on the other side of the door so it wouldn't open. It was the only kind she thought she could put on by herself and she knew no one in the house would help her.

In half an hour she was back. Motionless Papa was still enjoying his time spread out in the hallway, the note from her brother still tacked into his hand. Mary Rose held a hammer, a screwdriver and a knife. Two of the three she planned to use immediately.

She went into her room and, with great effort, secured the two hooks on the door, one at her eye level, one near the bottom. Then she moved her desk in front of the door. She arranged it so that she could sit at it to do homework and it would still block the door. Mary Rose did not plan to spend much time in any other part of the house.

Life as she knew it at home was over.

The past is always with you.
The past is always you.

The storm outside Meadow Lakes wasn't letting up. "Sometimes the sky just needs a good cry," Mary Rose McGill recited. The sky was crying along with her and she had not cried about this for years and years.

She remembered more.

She leaned back in her chair and fingered the cross again.

Hail Mary, full of grace.

She remembered how her mother had come home, calling out for her husband, then her son, then Mary Rose.

Mary Rose sat quietly at her block-the-door-desk, her book of Shakespeare in front of her, saying nothing.

"Where is everybody?" her mother yelled.

She was coming up the stairs.

The Lord is with thee.

"Surprise, surprise," Mary Rose thought to herself. She said nothing. She was totally still. She was silent when she heard her mother yell, "Oh My God!"

Blessed art thou among women.

Mama pounded on Mary Rose's door and tried to open it. "Mary Rose! Come help!" Mary Rose was silent. She didn't move.

Mama hurried to brother's room and yelled and pounded some more. "High Ho, Nobody Home," Mary Rose sang to herself. Mama rushed back down the stairs to the phone in the living room and called an ambulance, then she came back upstairs and pounded on Mary Rose's door again.

At first, she begged for help. Then she tried reasoning, forgiving, saying she knew Mary Rose was in there and that she didn't have anything to do with this terrible thing, then she threatened. Mary Rose looked at her clock radio. The ambulance was taking its time and that was fine with Mary Rose.

Trauma will do its thing. Mary Rose was still encased in plastic.

She didn't see or hear things clearly. She didn't feel. She just was. She looked at the locks on her newly locked door. One was a little crooked, but it didn't matter.

Finally, a siren.

Noises in the hallway.

"What's this on his hand?" one of the ambulance men asked. Her mother sounded confused. She hadn't seen brother's note.

She could hear them taking the man who had been her Papa down the stairs. She wondered if they bumped him as they went down. Bump, bump, bump; but now, they would have him on a stretcher. He would have gone bump, bump, bump, if she had dragged him down the stairs into the living room.

Shortly afterward a man's voice came through the door. "Young lady, you can come out now. It's safe. Your mom and dad are both in the ambulance."

Mary Rose waited.

The voice spoke again. It sounded kind.

They both waited.

Then the man pushed a card under her door. "If you need anything, just call us." The card had a police number on it.

Mary Rose waited.

She waited until things had been totally still for ten minutes by her clock radio, then she got up, pulled the desk out of the way, unlocked both locks and looked out. There was a big pool of blood in the hall.

Not her problem.

She went downstairs and into the kitchen. A baloney sandwich with pickles and mustard and a glass of milk would really taste good right now.

And So It Was –

That once again they gathered, this time, for the
first time, in Chaos' guest suite. It was really a little
studio apartment and she had made it home for
several months now. She had practiced potions and
spells, had passed on going to doctors with them,
had fainted when they discovered Winifred Wyttch's
body and had claimed no knowledge whatsoever of
the pillows that mysteriously changed chairs now
and then. Most importantly, she had made good
friends whom she would never forget, found a lot of
old-fashioned self-worth and love and been able to
say, "Darn!" whenever she wanted to do so without
being laughed at or even looked at in a funny way.

Life was good.

Alphonso had provided them with three bottles of
Two Buck Chuck Chardonnay from Trader Joe's,
along with some really nice cheese and crackers.
There were even five nice wine glasses on the tray
the server brought in.

Every chair in the apartment was in use. Marge
had her bad knee up on the hassock, Robbie was
sitting with one leg tucked under her, Hadley was
on the couch beside Chaos and Mary Rose was in
the one straight-back kitchen chair, her bare feet on
Geoffrey's big, soft side. He was sound asleep at her
feet, as usual, and now – also as usual – three white
rats in tiny sweaters were curled up around his ears.

Yes, life was indeed good.

The pillows on the ugly chairs in the lobby were on the correct chairs.

Chaos looked at them all and smiled. They were her family now, even though she would be leaving soon and would probably never see them again; or at least all of them again.

She placed a tiny recorder on the hassock by Marge's foot and said simply, "This okay?"

They nodded.

They were ready to tell each other, after nine years of friendship, who they really were.

"I'll go first," Marge said. "Nobody here knows I was a homeless teen."

They looked at her.

Mary Rose gasped a little gasp.

"I want to save mine until last," Robbie said. "It's of particular interest to our voodoo queen in training here." She smiled.

Mary Rose and Hadley looked at each other and did an eyeroll.

And Marge began - -.

Epilogue

Autumn had wrapped its arms around Meadow Lakes once again. Julie had changed the floral decorations to match the beautiful, huge trees outside with reds, yellows, browns and bronzes. The pillows on the chairs in the lobby had remained in place since before Chaos left.

Winnifred Wyttch's murder had been solved. Gum Shoue was in prison. All of them were relatively healthy and tremendously grateful for the friendship of women.

Chaos had texted them all a photo of herself with Double-Double, Toil and Trouble perched on her shoulders, proud in new sweaters. She was holding a pink vial. She had made it to Love Potion #6.

The girl was on her way.

It wasn't snowing as Robbie put on her favorite sleep shirt, the one with the bear holding a trowel and flower pot and the words "Hairy Potter" across the top. As the shirt slipped over her head, her cell phone rang. She knew the owner of that ringtone. The Good, the Bad and the Ugly meant Raven was calling. She laughed a sexy little laugh, pushed the green button and said, "Hello, Apache Man," then she took the phone, kicked off her slippers and settled into the bed for a long talk.

It wasn't snowing when Mary Rose McGill and Wiley Vondra settled into the couch at Mary Rose's apartment to listen to Classic Radio Shows. They had popcorn with M&Ms and Goldfish Crackers and sodas. Geoffrey was sprawled at their feet, serving as a warm, fuzzy foot stool. The announcer on the classic radio station was saying that Howard Duff would guest star as Sam Spade on this evening's George Burns and Gracie Allen's Hour, sponsored by Maxwell House Coffee, "good to the last drop." They looked at each other and smiled as George Burns said, "And that drop's good too." Wiley put his arm around Mary Rose, and, with the other hand, placed a yellow M&M in her mouth.

It wasn't snowing when Marge Aaron, dressed in her new black satin housecoat, opened her door for Alphonso Greatwood and the Mean Machine. She gave him a kiss on the top of his head, right in the center of his bald spot, as she took the bottle of expensive wine from the Mosel area of Germany from his outstretched hand. He turned, lifted his face to her and kissed her on the lips.

It wasn't snowing when Hadley Joy Morris-Whitfield put a steaming cup of hot cider and a plate with two chocolate chip cookies on the nightstand by her bed. She was dressed in a long white nightgown with matching bathrobe. Her tablet was in her hand, ready to dive into Drawn, a book by James Hankins, her favorite young author.

She had read that book once before, gone to his website and told him how much she liked it and he was kind enough to respond. They had developed an email relationship and she had joked that they were so much alike he must be the son who was stolen at birth. Now she would enjoy it again.

Hadley went to the bedroom window in her second floor apartment and looked out.

In the light illuminating the sidewalk around the property, she saw the first snowflake fall gently to the ground.

It was beginning to snow again.

Winter had returned to Meadow Lakes.

This is one of the pictures Robbie has in her album. Marie LaVeau was indeed, one of the most beautiful and powerful women of her time.

Marie's tomb. Today there are offerings and keepsakes left at the tomb asking for spells from the queen.

A Note from Joy

A lot has happened since the girls first met in 2009 and made Table 12 come alive for so many of us. I have ideas for **BOOB Girls X** and I hope to write it next year. They'll go to Alaska with Ted and me – provided we're still well and full of adventure. I have loved doing every book. Maybe you can come to the launch of that one – it will also be a birthday bash. My sweet husband, Ted Brown and I will both turn 80 in 2019.

After 50 pages, the girls begin to write each book and, as I say in the blog we write together, I really do think there is a Table 12 and a Meadow Lakes inside my old Toshiba.

I especially enjoyed two other women in the series – Anna Wilson, the madam of Omaha (**Book VII – Ten Little Puritans**), and the lady in this tale, the beautiful Marie Laveau, voodoo queen of New Orleans, who really did have a one-eyed snake named Zombi and a three-legged dog. We visited her tomb this year and I was reminded again of the delight of having a warped mind (mine) that admires these two – a woman whose brothel gave her most of downtown Omaha, and a magical force that still gets tokens placed at her feet. Esmeralda St. Benedict, the gypsy in book III is right there, too. Who among us does not wish for a little magic in our lives?

If I have dented anyone's copyright, I apologize. The photos Janet put in the book didn't have a copyright on them, so I assume we're Ok. Otherwise, I will apologize profusely and eat crow – but not at Marks Bistro. There, it's got to be Mac and Cheese.

As I write this, the musical, adapted by Fran Sillau with music by Mark Kurtz, hasn't yet premiered. Having those two suggest making the book into the play and then go with it, is a real honor. They're surrogate grandsons, and I love them both. I hope to see you on the front row, probably holding up a sign that says, *Never Underestimate A Burned Out Old Broad.*

If you think your local community theater would be interested in performing this delightful musical – with 20 songs – there is information in the back of this book.

A Special Thank You Love Potion from Chaos to:

❀ The first thanks goes to my genius daughter, Janet Roberts, who keeps Centering Corporation continuing as the oldest and largest bereavement center in North America and, especially, because she has created every cover in this series and amazed me with each and every one.

❀ Gloria Sorensen, retired librarian, deserves her own "Patience Potion" as my proofreader. I'm always super pleased when she misses a typo because I know she's gotten caught up in reading the story instead of watching for commas, doubles or other troubles. And if you find a typo or a bothersome piece of grammer - - blame Gloria. I swear that if I ever find an entire page without one of her red marks on it, I will frame it and give it to her gift-wrapped!

❀ A whole gallon of love potion to all of you who sent in ideas, suggestions and some truly tasteless plots. You are too many to thank individually, but you know who you are. This series is one of the few actually written in god part by readers and it just says again, *Never underestimate a burned out old broad.*

Hugs and lunch with Zombi and the three-legged dog for:

❀ My high school classmate and fellow author, Collen Hartman, who had supplied an idea for just about every BOOB Girls book, and who is the "realistic optimist" on page five. And to Jan Olsen, Slick Sheets, Susan Adams and others who were there when my emails arrived or the phone rang.

❀ Julie Carl, the florist of Meadow Lakes, purchased the right to be a character at the Ted E. Bear Hollow Comfort Food Classic. Julie invested a large donation, risking ridicule and typos to do a good thing.

❀ God love you, good friend Marge Rotherham, for the great toast at the wine party:
> "I don't drink much
> Two at the most
> Three, I'm under the table
> Four, I'm under the host."

❀ Ken Cousino has been my webmaster for theboobgirls.com, and my computer guru. Another million megs of hard drive for Ken, who can make my old Toshiba laptop talk like a new MAC. Ken inspired Ken David David in earlier books. Ken's wife, Denise, is a surrogate daughter who may end up taking care of me in my old age.

❀ He brings his own Love Potion, so I'm not giving any to my handsome husband, Ted Brown, who has packed more books, lifted more boxes, deposited more checks and shaken hands with and hugged more old ladies than he could have imagined. Ted takes good care of me and loves me to the moon and back. It's mutual and he inspired Raven in the last two books....except he's even better than Raven. When we were in New Orleans at Mardi gras, he was mistaken for Morgan Freeman. He reminds us that the group mistaking him had been drinking heavily for four hours.

❀ James Hankins is a terrific writer of thrillers that can be found on Kindle, Amazon, many libraries and through his website, Jameshankinsbooks.com, I thank James for plagiarize some of his best words. At least he knows I do so and I claim him as a son who was stolen at birth. For a good read after BOOB's IX, try *The Prettiest One, Shady Cross,* and *Brothers and Bones* as well as Hadley's favorite, *Draw.*

❀ There really is a Ron the Cop and big hugs and a pistol loaded with blanks go to Ron and Ursula Hall, who are good friends and pillars in The Compassionate Friends. Go for it, Officer!

❀ Fred Wilson gets a magical pillow from Chaos for actually having the mysterious switching pillows in the lobby of his retirement community. It's obviously voodoo.

❀ A shot in the eye back atcha to my real retinal specialist, Dr. Ed McGill, whose staff are huggers and fun and the epitome of good caregivers. And a hug in a heartbeat to the real Dr. Hottie, Dr. Art Easley, my cardio guy with a great staff and to Anne and Rebecca, super nurses. Anne is the one who daily goes from "prick to prick" in the cardio lab.

❀ She's already been called, "Porcelain on Steel" for her time at West Point, so it's a rare china tea cup with a drop of love potion to my minister and surrogate daughter, Rev. Cynthia Lindenmeyer, who taught me what it was like to be a homeless teen. I love you, Chaplain.

The BOOB Girls Tour –
where they've been in all the books

Wolf Brothers Western Store, where Wiley went to buy a new western sport coat, was one of my late husband Marv's favorite places to shop. Located at 70th and Dodge, it's an old Omaha landmark with great stuff.

Metropolitan Community College (Metro) where Ken David David is going and where he met Denise has several campuses, but the most beautiful is at 5300 North 30th Street and was actually the old Fort Omaha, built in 1868.

The Holland Center, where the gang went to hear the Omaha Symphony Pops concert, is at 13th and Douglas, an easy walk from the heart of the Old Market. The Holland is beautiful and has perfect acoustics. Two of my grandchildren have played there with the Omaha Area Youth Orchestra.

Prospect Hill Cemetery, where Anna Wilson and Dan Allen are buried is one of those best-kept secrets. Between 31st and 33rd Streets, bordered by Parker and Grant Streets, the cemetery hosts a reenactment each Memorial Day. It's a delight and the location is historic and beautiful. Residents of early Omaha used to picnic there on Sundays. It's worth a visit.

Nope, I'm sorry; there isn't a **Salem's Crossing, Nebraska.** Ben Schroeder, another surrogate grandson, loves Highway 30 so I let him set its location. He located it just North of Wood River which is two and a half hours west of Omaha just off I-80. Head there and you can see everything the girls saw and if you drive far enough, there's the Great Platte River Road Arch, Sandhill Cranes, Grand Island and America the Beautiful with amber waves of grain.

The Arboretum on Farnam Drive at 8141 Farnam, where I lived for three years, is just east of Methodist Hospital and, if you feel ambitious, you can park somewhere nearby and walk south on 84th Street to Pacific, turn right on Pacific and, in a short while, have coffee at **The Village Grinder.**

The Bookworm, where the girls browsed after coffee at The Grinder has moved. Get back on 84th, drive south to Center Street, turn right to 90th, then right again and you're at the new location. Go in and check to see how their supply of BOOB Girls books is holding up. The Bookworm is one of the finest independent bookstores you'll ever enjoy.

There really is a **Finicky Frank's** restaurant in Omaha and it's excellent. It's just off of I-680 at the 30th Street exit. Go north a very short way, turn left into a short road leading to the gas station and

Finicky's. My favorite thing there is the breaded pork loin.

If you are coming from West Omaha, go to 105th and Pacific, then turn south until you find the beautiful **Happy Hollow Country Club** where Hadley has taken the group in nearly every book. Unless it's lunch or dinner time, you can probably find Kelly or Jim to show you the library, the girls' favorite room. Dorothy, who had worked at "Happy" for many years, died a few years ago. The place will never be the same.

Drive on east to 72nd Street and turn left. Now you're at the area where Morgan Graves furnished La Viva Crypt from the **Lazy Leopard Lounge** auction.

Keep driving north to 72nd and Maple. Turn left and you'll be at **Centering Corporation** at 73rd Street. This is the grief resource center Joy and Dr. Marvin Johnson founded in 1977. Drive into the parking lot, come in and say hello. Inside is Caring Cups Coffee Stop. We're waiting for you. After a cup of good Joe, visit Benson Plant Rescue next door and wander through our memory garden where you will be shaded by one of the grandest and oldest cottonwoods in Nebraska.

You'll leave Centering, turn right, then make a U-turn to head east again on Maple. Drive by or stop in **Jane's Health Market** and **Leo's Diner** in the village of Benson.

Continue on to 49th Street and turn right. At the corner of 49th and Happy Hollow, the house on your right – a lovely little English Tudor – belonged to Joy and Marv for more than 30 years. Keep driving and you'll be at the **Homy Inn** where the girls went for champagne on tap. As you drive across Happy Hollow, look to your right. At the end of the block, by what is lovingly called the traffic peanut, is Dan Simpson's Auto Shop. Danny found the hidden tracker in the Hummer in BOOB Girls V.

If it's near lunch time, turn right at the Homy and go to the top of the hill to 51st Street. Turn left into the village of Dundee. Park where you can and walk to **Marks Bistro,** the girls' favorite restaurant at 51st and Underwood. If the weather is nice, have lunch on the most beautiful patio in Omaha. May I suggest Mark's famous Mac and Cheese, and ask for Mark. He'll be happy to say hello, show you Joy and Marv's booth – which is also Marge and her husband's - and the table where Warren Buffett met with Hillary Clinton.

After Marks, head south on 50th Street until you come to West Center Street. Turn left on Center and drive by **Kubat Pharmacy,** one of the few remaining family-owned pharmacies and where the girls bought the bedpan for Mary Rose's bedpan hat in BOOB Girls II.

Continue east on Center Street and you'll come to the **Old Market**. Now you're on your own. Visit Wheatfield's, The Jackson Street Tavern, M's and of course, Ted and Wally's Ice Cream. Stand beside the new Hyatt Place Hotel and look up at the third floor of the Mayfair Building across 12th Street. The apartment near the back by the fire escape was Joy and Marv's and Robbie's. You'll be standing where Esmeralda sang her sad song to Robbie, then patted the beautiful horse in BOOB Girls III. Go into the Passageway where Wes and Hadley had dinner and go smell the leather at Overland Sheepskin where Wes bought a jacket. Keep walking east and you'll come to the former ConAgra campus and lake.

If it's a nice day and you want to walk even more, the **Bob Kerry pedestrian bridge** across the wide Missouri is just a little way north.

Now drive back on Center Street to 84th Street. Turn left on 84th and go to **Mangelsen's**, where you can find just about everything you need, including help making a bedpan hat.

Go south to Interstate 80 by Mangelsen's and head west. Drive to the Springfield exit and head south to Louisville. There you'll visit **Coop de Ville** on

Main Street, the neatest little gift shop ever. Walk around the corner to the big white house and explore Feathers, the other gift shop decorated by Dr. Liz and her ladies. Have one of Dr. Liz's Scotcheroos and, like Robbie – buy a purse. It's sayings from the Coop bathroom that start the fifth book when Mary Rose looks in the mirror. "I do declare, I love my hair." That bathroom is worth a trip to Louisville anytime.

Get back on the highway by Louisville and drive a short distance to the sign reading South Bend. It's on Highway 66. If it's close to dinner time, head for **Round the Bend Steakhouse,** home of the Testicle Festival. Careful. Don't miss it, it's on your left and high on a hill.

After too much food at the Bend, go north until you get to I-80 again. Head west to exit 420. There is **Pine Grove RV Resort,** former home of Marv and Joy and where the girls went on their Staycation. Come in! Have a cup of coffee. Be sure to register at the office.

Go on to **Baker's Candies** in Greenwood and shop, shop, shop at the factory store. The gift shop is chocolate heaven.

You can dedicate an entire day to the **Henry Doorly Zoo,** where Marge and Alphonso had a date.

I'm sorry, but there is no **Meadow Lakes Retirement Community.** I picture it as being between Creighton University at 25th and California and the Old Market. There's no **Peyton's Hair Salon,** either. I picture it in one of the big apartment buildings near the river in the Old Market.

Ted and I are full time RVers at this time. We have a 34 foot motor home with three slide outs. One is a sunroom with four huge windows across the back, two on each side and four more in the ceiling. We call Omaha our home and, during the summer, we're at a place in Bellevue, Nebraska, called **Base Lake**, a very nice RV park that is part of Offutt Air Force Base. Ted was 25 years in the Air Force and one of my sweet pocessions is a big red travel mug that reads, Air Force Wife. Base Lake is hard to find, but if you do, coffee is on us.

I also imagine I've left out some places. If I have, remind me and I'll add them in the next book. Enjoy!

Cluck and Gobble Recipes

To start this off on the right foot (or wing or leg, as the case may be), we first need a lot of turkey or chicken meat.

I thought this sounded good! Here is a turkey recipe that also includes the use of popcorn as a stuffing ingredient -- imagine that. When I found this recipe, I thought it was perfect for people like me, who just are not sure how to tell when turkey is thoroughly cooked, but not dried out. Give this a try.

Turkey Recipe

8–15 lb. turkey
1 cup melted butter
1 cup stuffing (Pepperidge Farm is Good)
1 cup unpopped popcorn (ORVILLE
REDENBACHER'S LOW FAT IS BEST)
Salt/pepper to taste

Preheat oven to 350 degrees.
Brush turkey well with melted butter,
salt and pepper.
Fill cavity with stuffing and popcorn.
Place in baking pan making sure
the neck end is toward the front of the oven,
not the back.

After about 4 hours listen for the popping sounds.

When the turkey's ass blows the oven door open and
the bird flies across
the room,.... it's done.

And, you thought I didn't cook...

—Connie Johnk, Omaha NE

Refrigerator Chicken/Turkey Casserole

2-2/cups cooked & diced chicken or turkey
1 soup can milk
2 cups elbow macaroni, uncooked
1-3/4 cups chicken broth
2 cans cream of mushroom soup or may use cream of chicken soup.
1 small onion, chopped
1 can cream of mushroom soup
and one can cream of chicken soup
1 can 1 (5 oz.) can sliced water chestnuts
8 oz. shredded cheddar cheese
1/2 tsp. salt

Combine all ingredients. Pour into a well greased 9 x 13 inch pan. Cover with foil.

Refrigerate overnight until ready to bake. Bake at 350 degrees for 1 hour & 15 minutes.

–Julia Hughes, Alcester, S.D.

Bruschetta Chicken

1 can diced tomatoes, undrained
1 pkg Stovetop or similar type stuffing for chicken
1/2 cup water
2 cloves garlic, minced
1 1/2 lbs chicken cut into bite sized pieces
1 tsp dried basil
1 cup shredded mozzarella cheese

Preheat oven to 400 degrees. Place tomatoes in medium bowl with stuffing, garlic and water. Stir until stuffing is just moistened and set aside. Place chicken in 9 x 13 pan and sprinkle with basil and cheese. Top with stuffing mixture.

Bake 30 minutes or until chicken is cooked through.

–Joan Norman, Papillion, NE

Marilyn's Turkey Dish

4 cups turkey, cooked and diced
2 cans macaroni and cheese
2 cans cream of chicken soup
1 cup slivered almonds
1 can water chestnuts
1 pkg stuffing, sauteed in butter and put on top

Bake at 350 degrees for 30 minutes covered, then uncovered till brown.

–Marilyn Waugh, Ft. Collins, CO

Mary Rose McGill's
Yummy Biscuits and Bird Recipe

Mary Rose has been known to just buy a tube or two of biscuits and put them on the top of this dish.

1 c. chopped onion
1/2 c. butter, divided (1 stick)
1/4 c. dry sherry or water
1 (10 1/2 oz.) can low-sodium chicken broth
1 c. all purpose flour, divided
1 tsp. poultry seasoning
3/4 tsp. salt (optional)
3 c. chopped chicken breasts
1 (10 oz.) pkg. frozen peas and carrots, thawed
3/4 c. old fashioned oats, uncooked
2 tsp. baking powder
1/2 c. skim milk
1 egg white

Heat oven to 425 degrees. Cook onion in 2 Tbsp butter over medium high heat 3 minutes or until tender. Add combined sherry, broth, 1/4 cup flour, seasoning and salt; cook 3 minutes or until thickened. Stir in chicken and vegetables; pour into 2 quart casserole.

Combine 3/4 cup flour, oats, and baking powder. Cut in remaining butter until crumbly. Stir in milk and egg white until moistened. Drop 1/4 cupfuls onto chicken. Bake 38-42 minutes or until golden.

Hellmann's Leftover Turkey Casserole

4 cups leftover prepared stuffing, divided
4 cups coarsley chopped leftover cooked turkey
(about 1 lb.)
3/4 cup Hellmann's mayo
1/4 cup whole berry cranberry sauce
2 cups leftover mashed potatoes
1 1/2 cups shredded mozzarella cheese (6 oz)
scant handful dried cranberries

Preheat oven to 375. Spray 8 inch baking dish with nonstick cooking spray. Spoon in 2 cups stuffing, then top with turkey.

Combine 1/4 cup mayo with cranberry sauce, evenly spread over turkey. Combine remaining 1/2 cup mayo, potatoes and cheese in large bowl. Evenly spread on turkey, then top with remaining stuffing. Bake 40 min. or until heated through. Let stand 10 min. before serving. Garnish with dried cranberries.

–Jacque Miller, Omaha NE

Marge Aaron's Jailhouse Enchilada Chicken Casserole

2 C shredded cheddar cheese
2 C shredded Mozzarella cheese
2 Tbsp olive oil
1 large white onion diced fine
4 oz cab diced green chilies
1 can cream of mushroom soup
8 oz jar sliced black olives
4 lg flour tortillas, each cut into 6 pie-shaped wedges
1C your favorite salsa
3C diced cooked chicken meat

Preheat oven to 325 degrees F, and lightly grease a
9inch x 13inch baking pan.

In a small bowl, toss the grated cheese together and
set aside.

In a large frying pan, heat the oil over medium heat.
Add onion and sauté until soft.

Stir in the green chilis, soup and half the cheese.
Cook, stirring constantly, over medium-low heat until
the cheese melts.

Line the bottom of the prepared baking pan with
9 of the tortilla wedges. Spead evenly with 1/2 cup

of salsa. Cover evenly with 2 cups of chicken, then 1/2 the cheese sauce. Repeat the layers: first the remaining tortilla wedges, then salsa, then chicken, then cheese sauce. Top with the remaining shredded cheese. Bake uncovered at 325 degrees for 50 minutes or until hot and bubbly. Let stand on a wire rack for about 10 minutes.

Aunt Peggy's Turkey Casserole

2 c. shredded Cheddar cheese
2 cans cream of mushroom soup
3 c. Creamettes (uncooked)
2 small chopped onions
3 c. milk
3 c. cooked turkey
1 can cream of celery soup

Mix together and put in well buttered 13x9 inch pan. Refrigerate overnight.

Sprinkle with crushed potato chips just before baking the next day at 350 degrees for 1 hour.

–Cynthia Anderson, Akron, IA

Hadley Joy Morris-Whitfield's famous prize-winning chicken or turkey casserole

1 pkg stovetop dressing
3 C cooked chicken or turkey, cut up
Make dressing as on package
and place in 13 x 9 inch pan
Put chicken on top of dressing. Make custard:
½ Cup butter, ½ Cup flour, 4 C. canned chicken
broth, salt and pepper
Cook until thick.
Beat 4 to 6 eggs slightly. Mix small amount of custard
into eggs, then add remainder.
Pour over chicken. Sprinkle with paprika.
Bake 30-40 minutes at 350 degrees.
Let cool while you make the topping.

Topping: Heat: 1 can cream of mushroom soup, 1 cup
sour cream, 4 T milk, 1 can pimentos, chopped.
Cut casserole, pour topping over each piece. Garnish
with sprig of parsley if you wish.

Dr. Robinson Leary's Cajun Chicken Recipe Ingredients

10 ounces frozen chopped broccoli
4 cups cooked chicken
1 can condensed cream of chicken soup
1/2 cup mayonnaise
4 ounce can of mushroom stems and pieces, drained
3/4 cup grated Parmesan cheese

Cook broccoli according to package. Drain and spread in a 13x9 baking dish. Mix the cooked chicken, soup, mushrooms and 1/2 cup Parmesan cheese in a bowl. Spread chicken mixture over broccoli. Sprinkle remaining cheese over top. Cover with foil and bake at 350 degrees for 30 minutes. Remove foil and stir. Cover and bake an additional 15 to 20 minutes. May be covered and frozen for cooking at a later date.

About the Author

Joy Johnson Brown is nearly 80 now. With her late husband, Dr. Marvin Johnson she co-founded Centering Corporation, North America's oldest and largest bereavement resource center and Ted E. Bear Hollow, Omaha's center for grieving children. She is a nationally-known speaker and has written or edited over 100 books on grief, mostly for children.

Joy's three children, Jim, Jenny and Janet, all live near her in Omaha as do five of her six grandchildren, Jessica Joy, Paris Jennifer, Alex, Emma, Gregory and Liesel. Barney the Bernese Mountain Dog is now Janet's dog because Joy and her husband, Ted Brown, are full-time RVers, which allows her to present BOOB Girl talks all around the country. Ted brings five children and one grandchild to the new family they have created together.

If you enjoy this book,
you'll love and laugh with:

The Boob Girls: The Burned Out Broads at Table 12

The Boob Girls II: Lies, Spies and Cinnamon Roles

The Boob Girls III: Sandhills and Shadows

The Boob Girls IV: Murder at Meadow Lakes

The Boob Girls V: The Secret of the Red Cane

The Boob Girls VI: From the Eye of the Moose

The Boob Girls VII: Ten Little Puritans

The Boob Girls VIII: Learning to Love Willie

The Boob Girls IX: The Boob Girls in Training Bras

The Boob Girls X: Gospel Bird

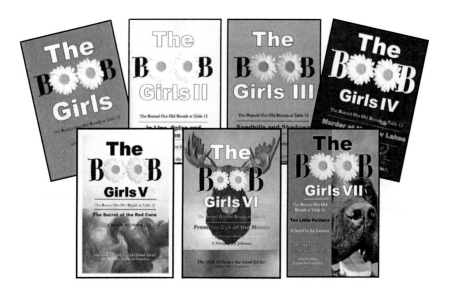

Now **YOUR** Community Playhouse Can Host
The BOOB Girls: The Burned Out Old Broads
The Musical

Now there is a new way to experience the delightful characters and offbeat adventures of "The Boob Girls." Adapted by innovative director and playwright Fran Sillau and award-winning composer Mark Kurtz, this musical comedy brings to the stage all the antics as well as tender moments from the book, along with exciting new songs, dances, and humorous entanglements. Your audiences will laugh till tears run down their legs.

The Tunes:

The BOOB Girl Theme
For the Rest of My Life, I'm Not Your Wife
None of that Kinky Stuff (Naked man in the Laundry Room Song)
It's Gonna Be Good: The Shopping Song
Just Look at Us and Beautiful
No Forwarding Address
Extortion is Sweet
Freedon!
The Family You Found
The Tattoo Song
I'm in Love with J Frederick Sapp
Argument
Polly's Song
The Adult Emporium Song
Wes and Hadley's Song
All Heart – the Hospital Song
We'll Remember
The BOOB Girl Song

For information about how your theater can produce this crowd-pleasing musical, please contact fran@fransillau.com.

Visit the girls and Joy Johnson at:

www.theboobgirls.com

www.welcometothe boobgirls.blogspot.com

Bring Some Joy to Your Group

Joy Johnson Brown speaks to over fifty groups each year with a humorous presentation on The Making of A BOOB Girl. Contact her for your state, national or local conference or meeting at joy.johnson@msn.com or through her website at www.theboobgirls.com.

To speak to her by phone, contact Centering Corporation at 866-218-101.

BOOB Birds Print Full Color
Unframed, 18x24
$25

Order from www.theboobgirls.com

or

www.centering.org

Phone: 1-866-218-0101